FIRE IN THE PINES

FIRE IN THE PINES

STEVEN FRANSSEN

stevenfranssen.com

twitter.com/stevefranssen

youtube.com/c/stevenfranssen

To all the cowboys.

Table of Contents

Part One

    The first drone I saw was the same afternoon all the cell phones stopped working. It was flying low across the valley toward the military depot. No cage on the underside. My father, brother, and I took the trail down on our horses and spied the depot with Dad's rifle scope. The military draft had taken most of the young men out of the valley. We saw a few of them now, loading up into aerial transports, some of them into trucks. Most of the faces we didn't recognize, however. Dad waved to another man on a nearby ridge who was watching the depot as well. They were both "draft dodgers", as the government people in town called them. The warrant for Dad's arrest had only been out for a couple of weeks at this point. It didn't seem to matter too much to the sheriff's department since they didn't have a budget to go out and find him. Nobody but my father and a few other mountain people seemed to have any money to do anything. I didn't believe my father when he first told me that it had always and forever been the other way around: the government people had all the money and made all the rules.

    The soldiers took off on in the direction of Bozeman. There was a big airlift out of there. We never saw any of those men again. Soon there were no more lights at night from most of the villages and towns in the valley. The sky was grey within a week and the ashes started so many wildfires, the valley was encased in smoke for the rest of the summer. Our home was next to a river and up a rocky draw. With a natural breeze going through, we were spared the worst of it.

Dad came back home with us the day the soldiers left. He said the sheriff wouldn't come now. We were delighted. My brother got off the horse we shared and rode with our father. I felt happy for him as I looked back now and then to see them on the trail behind me. Dad was coming home after being away for two weeks, staying nights in our neighbor's hay loft.

After a long embrace, my parents spoke for a while.

"Better go stock up before it turns to looting," said my mother. "Are you and Russell going into town?"

"Just for the medication and some gas," he responded.

Russell was our neighbor. He had two boys. I was close friends with them. He and his wife had come to the valley a few years ago but had managed to establish themselves quite nicely.

"Are you taking Jim?" she asked, referring to me.

"What do you think, son?" my father winked as he asked me. We left as soon as Russell showed up with his oldest son, Dale.

We rode into town in the diesel pickup. The gas station owner had left a sign in the window saying, "Good luck" and all the dispensers were wide open. With a population of around five hundred, we weren't in a lot of competition from other folks from the valley. The back of the pickup was loaded down with 55-gallon drums of diesel fuel by the time we were done.

We headed further into town and saw other people for the first time. They were walking into one of the half-dozen stores in town that had supplies of any kind. We waved to them and they waved back. I had seen enough movies for this to be at odds with my expectations of what a societal collapse would look like. My father, too, had anticipated it would be a lot worse than this.

We stopped outside the sporting goods shop that had a small grocery store in the back. I stayed with Russell and Dale while my father stepped in to get groceries and ammo. We had stores and stores of these things back home but this would be one of the last opportunities to get fresh produce, perhaps for a long time. My father told us to keep the pickup running at all times. I wasn't sure why.

I began to peer into the shop window to see how empty the shelves were when the reflection of Sheriff Gates' patrol car came into view. He was a hundred feet away when he stepped out of the patrol car. I noticed Russell pull back the hammer on his revolver as quietly as he could. He beckoned us to step back from the pickup and away from the fuel.

Gates noticed our movement and called out, "It's fine." He took his badge from his lapel ceremonially and set it on the hood of his vehicle. Russell relaxed a little when Gates followed up with, "I'm not after him. That's not the deal anymore," referring to my father.

"Why?" asked Russell as Gates approached, keeping his hands far and away from his service piece.

"The Internet went down this morning. The media was saying there were nukes going off in Oregon, Washington, and maybe here in Montana. Whatever they wanted to pull your friend into has already kicked off. Take care of yours now, Russ."

My father came out to ask Gates if he was going to arrest him. An answer in the negative came and he went back in to fetch two baskets filled to the brim with ammo for a pistol caliber he was after. "Jim's giving most of it away," he said to the two other men. "Says he doesn't need it and we're welcome to it."

I could tell just how on-edge my father and his friend were around the sheriff. The media said that dodging the draft was toxic and racist. A lot of people in the region still believed what the media said. Sheriff Gates agreed only until his job and paycheck were no longer secure. There was some more small talk before the man went in to the store to get what he needed for himself.

Just then a man in a large military style vehicle drove slowly by with his window down.

My father smiled and pointed, saying, "Look son, there he goes!"

Dale and I waved to Kevin Tedrick, the old movie star, and he waved back. He owned the Big Country Ranch on 10,000 acres just under an hour away. He was loved in our area for starring in some of the last Western movies Hollywood eked out. About the most excitement our town got was when he'd convince some higher-up to film scenes in the area. A few older people I knew had gotten work as extras.

The movie star rounded the bend and drove over a hill, out of sight.

Activity in town was picking up as more and more people realized what was going on. We were in the feed supply store when the backup power generators switched on. The power grid had gone down. The atmosphere began to intensify. We paid with silver and left with various bags of minerals and animal related remedies. By this point, this was the busiest I had ever seen our town. Few people were in cars, which was strange to behold. Lots of people on foot and some with horses. Everyone was gathering what they could. At most there was a bit of pushing and stern words passed but everyone knew everyone else. There was a sense of purpose to the whole scene. The previous year there had been a general trucker strike for all the distributors that went through our part of the valley. No new food came through for a week. Prices skyrocketed and a lot of trust was lost. This was different. We were in for "the big one".

As we drove out of town, a shootout started. The air cracked with heavy rifle fire. Dale and I looked in the direction of the shot and then looked at each other. My father said, "There it is," knowingly, over the throb of the diesel engine. Some weeks later we learned it was people of different colors that had hated each other for a long time finally getting into it.

The summer passed with the sky growing darker and darker. A thin layer of ash settled in some places to the north of us where the valley opened up onto the fields. One night in late October, after weeks of total silence, all of the lights in the valley went out, including ours. This confused my father and Russell because we were on our own power system. This happened every two weeks through winter. Fewer and fewer lights throughout the valley would come back on. My father went out on his horse to see what he could find out but other than finding a few families burning a whole lot of firewood, he found nothing out of the ordinary. No one had any leads or any information. All of the supplies in the valley were snapped up and there were no public meetings. The only thing that was certain was that anyone who drove toward Salt Lake or Billings never came back. Not a single one. We were boxed in by some unseen force and cut off from communication to the outside by some kind of scrambling across the entire radio spectrum.

The deep snow dulled our curiosity about the outside world and we settled into a wonderful rhythm at the cabin.

Russell and his wife, Anne, would bring their boys over and we'd all spend the time doing chores, preparing food, or playing games. My job was to feed the meat rabbits we kept in the barn. I loved the rabbits and had names for all of them. My sister, Wendy, helped me when it was time to change their bedding or clean out their pans. Richard, my brother, tagged along and watched us. He contented himself to petting the rabbits but the chickens he helped out on, too. At nine years old, he was two years my junior and twice as headstrong. He was never satisfied with explanations. He was the type to find out for himself. We were reminded of this when, after warned not to dump anything nasty into the river so that neighbors wouldn't get sick, he not only urinated in the river but walked down to the neighbor's place to ask them how the water tasted. Richard wanted to learn on his terms and was ferociously attuned to his own path in life.

Wendy was the same as my mother. She was intelligent and devoured books like they were nothing. She was also sweet and attentive to my brother and I the way our mother was to our father. She concerned herself with our interests and ambitions, which mostly lay in taking our games around the house to another level. Richard and I challenged her to be independent from us, pushing her away if we could but she didn't mind much. She led us with her quiet countenance and we respected her for it.

My father, Frank, had a terrible hunch long before he moved us to the Valley. He was living in the most conservative, reasonable city he could find for my sister and mother. The place was going downhill fast and that's how he knew to put more stock in the doomsayers than some of his more reasonable, balanced friends had. He was involved politically for a time, helping out on the campaigns for decent people who wanted to turn back the clock on the madness that was accumulating. I didn't get to see my dad work out in the world. All that was a part of his former life where he survived by his wits and kicked any extra he made into investments. Those investments were enough to bring our family to the valley to live on a good piece of land. He was semi-retired from that point forward. When we first lived in the valley, people sought him out for advice. By the time of the collapse, we had maybe two visitors a year outside of Russell and his family. People my father knew in the cities would write to tell him he was paranoid and had given up the fight too early. This bothered him only slightly. He considered these people disloyal and cut them loose. He took no joy in the idea that he had proven them wrong.

My father was a tall, broad-shouldered man. His eyes had a piercing intensity that suggested his mind was always churning on something. In his youth he had thirsted for action but since I was born, he contented himself to raising us. He dedicated his strength to our betterment. We loved playing with him. He wrestled us, provoked our imaginations with all manner of stories, and took us for long walks in the woods to discuss what we were learning. He and my mother delighted in one another's company but also maintained a serious working relationship that kept the household efficient. I marveled at his attention to detail and the long hours he would put in when a project on the property was conceived.

When spring first came, we sheared all the sheep and the angora goats with hand shears. My mother kept a lot of it but we used the rest as an excuse to go and barter with whomever we could. For four months we had only had contact with Russell and his family. Our pantry was still loaded with canned goods and so far, no one had come by for food, begging or otherwise. Most people completely missed our cabin as the long driveway to it looked like a logging access road thanks to the gate from a county auction my father had put in the way. We were starved for some society, some measure of togetherness with people in the valley. We knew an older couple, Terry and Sue. We figured we could see them. They were like family. Everyone pitched in and we cleared our shared road down to where the paved part of the old county road met with the two other roads in the area. The work took us the better part of two days. Nobody wanted to wait another month until the snowmelt hit our elevation. Russell and his oldest son Dale, my father and I loaded into my father's old diesel pickup. We sat in the bed of the pickup with wild anticipation of what we might see.

"Do you think a lot people died?" asked Dale. He had started puberty a number of months before I did and to me, his voice sounded deeper than mine could possibly ever be.

"I don't think so. Everyone here is tough," I responded.

"Then where is everyone?"

The three farms we had passed on the county road so far had been empty. Not a trace of people outside and all the livestock we were accustomed to seeing were gone.

"They're probably with their families somewhere," I suggested. I pulled the .22 caliber revolver my father let me carry from its holster and joked to Dale, "If they turned into zombies, we'll just have to shoot them!"

He laughed and showed me the 9mm pistol his father let him carry. It bothered me that he could carry a more powerful caliber. When I turned 12 in May I would be allowed to carry "the big guns" as my father promised. I thought it was unfair because Dale had been allowed to carry large calibers for two years now. I think my father was over careful because he did not want to give my brother and I a penchant for violence.

We were almost to town when we saw our first people. We slowed down when we saw them.

"Howdy," the older of the two men said in a non-committal tone. The two of them were setting some fencing back into place outside of what looked to be an auto body shop.

"How was your winter?" my father asked.

The younger one replied, "Not too bad. A bit hungry. Yourselves?"

"Oh, not bad," said my father. I could tell he was unsure of these guys. He had only ever used the other mechanic in town and these guys had a lazy reputation.

They made some small talk for a while longer. The younger of the two men asked whereabouts we had come from and my father lied to him, telling the man we were living on a different road than the one we lived on. This set me on edge. I wasn't sure why. There was something unknowable about these men. There was an uncertainty in our existence that hadn't been tested until this moment. For months we had persisted up our draw, on the river with people we trusted down to the bone. The harshness of the world suddenly loomed closer than it had ever been my whole life. The men looked gaunt. One of them glanced into the bed of the pickup. I think he was looking for food. My father kept the engine running the entire time and when conversation trailed off, we got going.

We drove a loop around town. A young woman came out to our vehicle as we slowly passed through her neighborhood. She begged us for food. I recognized her as a waitress from the restaurant we went to for Wendy's birthday the previous summer. The woman was much prettier then. She was thin now, too thin. My dad sped up as she got closer to the pickup. She sat down in the middle of the street with a dejected look on her face. I felt pity for her and tossed out a bag of peanuts I had been keeping, out onto the street. A different woman sprinted from out of nowhere and beat the young woman to the food, causing her to cry loudly. My father had warned me people in town would be hungry and some of them would be desperate. We got to the far edge of town and were shocked to see the retirement home had burnt to the ground. Everyone's cars were still there. Eerie thoughts passed through my head.

"Do you think everyone was inside?" I asked Dale.

He nodded and looked away.

We turned onto the old highway to take a more roundabout way home. We stopped at Terry's house. Terry was a retired realtor. Terry was like my father, a man who had made his money elsewhere and chose the valley as his last stand. His property was impressive. His driveway was much longer than ours and lined with old growth trees from a farmer who owned the place fifty years prior. In a move that neighbors gave him grief for, Terry had chosen to erect a stone wall along his portion of the old highway. His neighbors stopped talking to him altogether when he affixed broken glass across the top of the wall. The river that ran by our house forked out into three creeks, one of them passing through the front of his property and under a bridge at the halfway mark of his driveway. His Caucasian shepherd, Bear, came barking up to the side of the truck as we drove along. His tail wagged in excitement. Dale threw a piece of beef jerky to him. He followed us the rest of the driveway as it curled around a barn and placed us at the back of Terry's house. This was a second home for me. My parents renewed their wedding vows in a ceremony under a gigantic willow tree nearby. Terry's wife, Sue, was standing on the back porch when we hopped out of the pickup. We greeted her with hugs. She beckoned us to come inside as Terry was doing some work down in the basement. The four of us went down the basement steps and were met by the sound of woodworking. Terry stepped away from a bench lined with chisels, files, clamps, and a great number of other tools I had little frame of reference for. From the looks of it he was gluing slats of wood together to cut them into some kind of unique piece. This work interested me some but it was something Terry did only on rare occasion.

After greeting us all, Terry asked where my younger brother was. He was fond of my brother. When my siblings and I visited Terry, he gave Richard most of the eye contact. He liked Richard because Richard was "stubborn as an ox". It was a trait Terry prized in his own brother, who had passed away many years before in a drunk driving accident.

Conversation quickly moved back up to the kitchen where Sue served us tea. I didn't like mine and I noticed Dale putting extra sugar in his. The men moved from chitchat to a discussion of the coming year and what could possibly be happening out in the world.

"Jose and Santiago aren't coming back," said Terry of his ranch hands who had been with him for over a decade. The two men had left early in the summer the previous year because of political unrest and waves of violence in Mexico. They had families to take care of and enough savings over the years with

Terry that they were cashed out handsomely upon their departure. My father expressed his concern that one or both of them had been caught up in the ethnic conflicts that were sweeping the Southwest. I listened closely to this kind of talk. I wasn't sure why it interested me. My brother and sister were more content to know about what was most immediate to them. I liked the abstract most. There was a governor of one of the southwestern states who commanded enough loyalty from the people there that when the dollar crashed, he sent in troops to commandeer strategic military bases. He only succeeded because this happened in several US states. A decent sized bulk of the country had stayed intact, mostly because of the efforts of a populist out of Kansas who flexed his might against these tyrants. He kept America's access to ports open on the west coast by carving a bloody path through Nevada and California. This kept the bulk of the Pacific fleet in America's hands and provided an eroding bulwark against China's colonization of western Canada and the Pacific Northwest. Those regions had broken away and formed socialist governments in league with China, as much as was possible. I remember going to Seattle when I was four and seeing an Asian city. My father explained the similarity of this city to ones over in Asia by showing me pictures and telling me about what happens when lots of people move from one place to another.

Terry riffed on his surprise that no one came back from trips down south to Salt Lake City. The leaders of the Mormon church also participated in the break-up of America but while everyone veered to socialism, Utah stayed on its own course as a business and family friendly place. Much of the economy in our area was because of trade with the Mormons. They called their nation Deseret but it was the church elders that were in charge of everything. The Church there had been smart by acquiring nuclear assurances long before. They were spared a lot of the bloodshed that much of the continent had seen. This was why it was so confusing that people disappeared when they left for Salt Lake. The point of no surprise, particularly to Russell who had worked over there, was that anyone who ventured too far west into Washington state was charged as a criminal, imprisoned for a short term, but allowed to return, albeit with a prison tattoo. They were collecting people's DNA. There was a border dispute between our nation, the Rocky Mountain Federation, and China's colonies in that region. Terry gave us the latest updates he'd heard from people passing through on the old highway. There were huge swaths of the continent without power. Commerce was grinding to a complete halt because of hyperinflation and a lack of production. The rumor was that millions were dying in the major cities. There were diseases released by the governments to kill each other's citizens. Without fail, any place that had electricity would lose it for a day or two at a time, every two weeks. Then whole regions lost power altogether. I thought about the potential for aliens deciding they wanted to take over the planet and the movies I had seen where this was attempted. The basic point Terry drove home was that something had finally flipped for the people who held the most power and we no longer lived in a world where the will of the people mattered. He indicated it had everything to do with the diseases that were spreading and clandestine technologies that had come to see the light of day. I believed it. My parents had wanted a fourth child and were young enough to have one. They lamented to us many times over the years that they wanted more siblings for us. My father was bitten by something on business trip he had taken to Washington D.C. He fell deathly ill, especially in his lower intestines and groin. The doctors said that the disease had made him infertile. This happened to millions of people just before the economy collapsed. Russell and his wife, Anne, had only managed to have two children, despite trying for the entirety of Anne's thirties to have a third. Terry said it was all part of a plan that was now being executed by wicked, intelligent people in the highest halls of power. He had books about things that weren't on the Internet, no matter how much you searched. I looked at those books sometimes but they frightened me. They were imbued with some kind of malevolent power that I wanted nothing to do with. He also had a series of portrait photographs framed in the office he used to use when he was a realtor. They were all people he considered patriots, heroes, and intellectuals who fought for freedom. Most of them were dead or imprisoned. My father had worked with one or two of them but always behind the scenes.

Russell and Terry smoked tobacco from pipes as we toured Terry's livestock. The ugly scenes back in town came back to mind when we saw a man go by on a dirt bike on the old highway some distance away. I mentioned this to Terry. He was none the wiser about the retirement home burning to the ground. There had been a few beggars at his gated wall but they lost the stomach for their designs when Bear and Moose, Terry's St. Bernard, came snapping their jaws and barking loudly. There were much easier marks in the area for foragers and thieves. As it was a wealthy area for out-of-towners, many people were caught in the cities and had been unable to make it to their mountain retreats. Terry mentioned running into Kevin Tedrick on the large eighteen-hundred-acre parcel of public land that separated their properties, sometime in November while the hunting was still good. The public land focused into a wedge that divided their properties by only a stone's throw. Kevin was a widower and kept to himself but Terry had done outfitting work for the movie star when they had both been much younger. Kevin's son and his wife were living up at the lodge with him. They were expecting a child in the late summer. Terry had gone up to the lodge to see them. This news excited me and I wondered if Kevin would ever be in movies again. Or perhaps his son would as the man was the spitting image of his father and was still quite young.

We stopped outside a pen where two hogs were resting in the cold mud.

"It's not going to get better this year," warned Terry. "I don't know much but I do know there are bad people north of the valley doing awful things. Trouble will come our way. Tedrick knows people. They want him in on what they're doing.

They said they wouldn't bother him if he said 'no'. He's hedging his bets."

"What are these bad people doing?" asked Russell.

"I don't know. He wouldn't tell me. Whoever sent feelers his way means business."

I could tell this troubled my father. He sent Dale and I to go check on Terry's chickens while the men continued the conversation. Dale and I watched from a distance and were left without many clues as to the nature of their discussion. Dale's attention wandered and I decided to leave with him to go throw rocks in the creek.

There were mule deer grazing near an apple tree. It was almost the beginning of summer down here in the valley, or at least it felt like it. I thought of a burrito feed one of the churches nearby held every year around this time. The congregation was made up of old folks so we were treated like celebrities, my siblings and I, any time we stopped by for an event. My parents didn't take us there regularly but when they held events we would show up. I think my dad wanted to bolster them somehow. He often lamented the lack of young parents in the valley. He said everyone was taxed too much. We were at a building supply store once in Butte, tracking down some metal roof panels my dad wanted, when a Somalian family with seven children went by with a cart. He cursed the man and told them they weren't welcome in America. These kinds of confrontations happened all the time in the bigger towns in Idaho, Wyoming, and Montana but they never went past that, like in the big cities. In those places there were gangs, separated by ethnicity and warring with each other. In the valley there were two militias and they kept anyone who wasn't white from settling in the valley. All of the police were members and word was that some of the military guys were sympathetic, too. But longstanding landowners of other races were allowed to stay. I think some trouble came out of that.

Terry kept a lot of his firearms in sealed irrigation pipes by the chicken coop. Terry never let it on. My father told us about the cache, saying that it was to fool the military. The military used to fly jet black helicopters over the area with large devices attached to their undercarriages. These were ground penetrating radar systems. When the Internet wasn't blocked off, we saw a lot of alternative media stories come out about gun bans and confiscations. A lot of people figured it would happen here and it worried me for a time. Once the military base cleared out, I hadn't given it a second thought until seeing Terry's irrigation pipes. Dale caught my glance and gave me a look like he knew that I was thinking about the guns in the pipes. We fed the chickens and wondered to ourselves if we should clean out the coop as it smelled like hell.

A giant drone zoomed overhead, flying low before whipping up and over the tree line on the way to Kevin Tedrick's ranch. We hit the dirt and watched it fly out of sight. Two concussive sounds erupted, followed by large explosions some distance away. We crawled toward the irrigation pipes, hoping we could pop one open. Terry roared into the area in my father's pickup and called out to us. We hopped on and went back to the farmhouse where Sue took us down into the basement. My father, Russell, and Terry left on an armored four-seater Terry kept for such an occasion. They were armed to the teeth. I watched them head out into the field and beyond the tree line toward the sound of the explosions.

Sometime later they came back with a wounded man strapped to the back of the four-seater. It was Kevin Tedrick! Sue rushed up to help the men as they loaded Kevin into the room outside the meat cooler where the animals were slaughtered. They heaved Kevin onto the big table and I saw clearly how his chest and legs were torn and bloody. He was unconscious and bleeding from his head.

Sue was trained as a nurse and the men deferred to her as she set to work on Kevin, patching him up as best she knew how.

An alarm howled and Terry yelled for us to get down. An explosion rocked the house and I heard the rush of a drone ripping through the sky. A large gap had been blown into the roof of the house that we could see out of.

"Stay down," Terry yelled as he and my father went into another room. Kevin was coming to. He had a grim look in his eyes. A drone screamed through the air. Terry rushed back to where we were and pointed a large tube into the air. With a loud rush of air, a rocket blasted from the tube and into the sky. We heard an explosion.

"Get the second one. There's two," Kevin grunted as he sat up.

I could see my dad outside with the second launcher. He fired it at something much farther away and soon enough we heard the explosion.

"Good," said Kevin as he rested on his elbows before sliding back into a supine position. His eyes closed but his breathing was regular. Sue continued to work on him, focusing on the heavy bleeding that was forming down his leg. "Milo and Caroline are fine," he muttered before passing out.

An hour later we had already dug up one of Terry's weapons caches and left the farmhouse for a cabin Kevin kept hidden in a thicket of trees beneath a rocky outcropping I had never been to. His son, Milo, met us with medical supplies. He brought his pregnant wife with him. The new supplies had stopped Kevin's bleeding altogether.

"They're not at the lodge," said Milo.

"Who's 'they'?" asked Russell.

"There's a socialist outfit in Missoula trying to muscle me out of the valley," said Kevin.

"They're more than 'socialist'," Milo said sternly to his father.

"Not in front of the boys," said Milo's wife, Caroline.

"It's fine," said my father. "They know things are going to get much worse. We've prepared them for it."

Kevin looked at Russell to confirm and then said, "They're secret society types. The ones who've had surgeries."

I remembered my father telling me about how in some parts of the world there were secret society people starting to operate out in the open. At first, they were offering hungry families money for their children and promising better lives for the children. When the famines were really bad, just before the grid went down, a video came out of a man who had had surgery to look like a woman. He was flaying a child with a whip. My dad wouldn't tell me what else was in the video. They made those videos to send people into a panic.

"They're the ones who forced me to retire. They were more powerful before the fall. The few soldiers who were at the Air Force base in Spokane cleared out and these people…"

"Say their name," said Milo.

"The Progressive National Committee," said Kevin. "Let's call them 'commies.'"

"They're more than commies," Milo interjected once again. "Come on, Dad."

"They're satanic pedophiles," said Terry, leaning against a huge timber column with his arms crossed. "We call *them* 'satanics'. Or we don't call them anything at all cause they're easy enough to spot." Instinctively I put my hand on the small revolver I was carrying. Dale and I made eye contact. Sue noticed and gave us a pained look.

"Their cult goes back thousands of years," said Kevin. He grimaced and said, "They wanted me to join their rituals. At first, they were giving me good business deals and the more I earned their trust, the stranger things got. The gender-crossed ones are higher in the hierarchy. I started meeting more of them. I didn't like it and pulled out of a deal the day after I was invited to a ritual. They blacklisted me from Hollywood, talked to the big studio heads they control. I did a Christian movie or two toward the end there but they stopped the release by buying out the production company."

"They came on my land before the fall," said Terry. "Just two of them, in business suits. Strange looking bastards. They were interested in the fresh water spring in the lee beyond the grazing fields. Their aerials were as good as they got. I showed them out."

Frank, my father, said, "I didn't know they were the ones looking at all the fresh water. They put a bid on the irrigation district but nothing came of it."

"They're headquartered in Alberton," said Kevin. "There's just a few of them. I've been there for business. They're after me because they don't trust that I'll keep quiet about their facilities. They're idiots. Nobody's coming for them. There's no government anymore. Nukes are still going off in the cities. Everyone's at each other's throats. There's no oversight. Only Deseret and the Reformed States are worth a damn, at this point. I thought they'd leave me alone but they keep wanting to cut me in. They know how much I've got up here."

"They want to control the valley," observed Terry.

"Everyone's dead in Missoula and Helena," Kevin said heavily. "A Chinese outfit controls Spokane. Preppers control Kalispell. They have enough to be dangerous but not enough to muscle out anybody else. South is the only way they have to go. They have another compound down in Central Idaho. They probably want to link up and figure I'm in the way. Well, I guess I am."

"You're the biggest fish around," said Milo.

"They sent their message. They destroyed my hangar. I'm down to a drone and some horses. It's my best drone, though."

"We got two of theirs," my father said proudly.

"We sure did," said Kevin.

I could feel everyone in the spacious cabin hanging on his every word. He was a natural born, reluctant leader. He was the hometown king even though he was born and raised in Iowa. He pitched in the minors for a while and all the cowboy movies he'd done brought a lot of money into our valley. Nobody wanted to come here as America was falling apart because there's no watershed here, so a lot of local families ended up with the time to get secure before the fall.

"How strong are they?" asked Russell.

"They have maybe another two drones at most. Maybe a dozen guards on site. A lot of people shuffled in and out of their compound when things were still up and running. I can't imagine there are many people going there now. A lot of them were in Helena when the nuke dropped."

"Should we go after them?"

"On account of who they are, I'm inclined to say yes," said Kevin. "They probably think I'm dead. That's an advantage. They'll probably try to move their operations into the valley and then down into Idaho with their pals. After a long winter they're looking for fresh blood. But they're weak. They're weak as fuck. Down south they're much stronger."

Shivers went down my spine. I knew I wasn't in danger so long as my father and Russell were nearby. I felt a desire to kill, which was a new experience.

"There were parades for these people not much more than a year ago," said Sue. "Won't there be reprisals? They had a lot of support."

"The only support they had was government support and all of those folks were blasted to smithereens," her husband replied.

Milo's wife brought Dale and I glasses of water to drink. I marveled at how shiny the crystal of the glass was. Kevin had spared no expense.

"We'll come with," my father offered up his and Russell's support.

"I'll watch over your families," Terry immediately replied. "Sue and I will go up to them."

My father nodded in agreement. "You fit to ride?" he asked Kevin.

"Give it a day or two," said Kevin. "Your boys coming with?"

"Please…" I pleaded with my father.

"They'll come. They'll stay with the horses when we get there."

"We're gonna kill em'," said Kevin. "Those kinds of people shouldn't exist."

"You had to hold back when the government was still running everything," Terry said with spite. "Free range now. They deserve every bit of it, trying to terrorize the valley like this."

I liked the talk of killing. It was new to me yet it felt very familiar. I didn't think Kevin was playing a character from one of his movies. This felt more immediate than that, it was personal somehow.

"The boys will stay with the horses," Kevin repeated my father's edict. He stepped gingerly into the room I considered to be his study. We all waited quietly as he rustled some drawers. I heard the whir of an electronic lock and a large door opened. He came back into the great room with a drone two feet across. "This'll scramble their security systems when we get there."

I thought about the cameras I had seen mounted on the sides of the cabin and how one of them had kept its lens pointed directly at me wherever I stepped. I marveled at how much access to electricity Kevin must have had.

Terry and Sue left that night for my house to look over my mother and siblings and Russell's family. We wished them well. They took my father's pickup so the diesel drums could be brought home. Dale and I were surprised to see Milo and his wife leave. We thought Milo would be coming with us. His kid was due at later in the year. The kid was his first and he wanted to take no chances. They went to Kevin's home in Idaho, not far away. The man was so rich, I couldn't hardly fathom it. In the cabin there were pictures of him with lots of wealthy conservative men: famous politicians, ranch owners, businessmen, and a few elderly celebrities from a time when Hollywood "wasn't gay", as Kevin put it. I felt comforted by the pictures, like it was some kind of lost fraternity that Dale and I belonged to but couldn't join. These men seem imbued with a mystical quality that sent my mind peeling back through the generations. I couldn't help but connect the scene to all the portraits of great men that Terry kept. There was some tradition there. All of that was lost. Kevin was magnetic for a reason. He not only knew the secrets of the satanic types but the secrets of the best men.

The next night we sat at the fireplace and listened to Kevin, my father, and Russell talk late into the night.

"I've been saving up some terrible violence," said Russell. "I don't like it but it's what needs to be done.

Russell was chewing a bit of tobacco. He spit into a bronze bowl Kevin had brought over from the kitchen. He only did this when my father and him were slaughtering pigs or goats. Under normal circumstances, he kept it pretty clean.

"I got so damn tired of those demons when they were plastered all over the media," my father said in agreement. "The violence I don't like. It's just what is necessary."

"They ran everything before the fall. I wouldn't be able to tell you the half of it," said Kevin. "They were giving kids hormones to speed them up. You sure it's alright to say in front of the boys?"

My dad said it was fine. He and Russell were dressed in Kevin's western wear. He had kept a lot of his movie wardrobe in the cabin, thinking it would mostly serve as a place to smoke cigars and drink brandy with movie stars and musicians who passed through the area. My dad looked like a regular cowboy.

"Children with beards and all kinds of craziness," Kevin said reluctantly. "There was a pool party they had me go to when I was in talks for a picture for one of their studios. I left early. Said I was sick. They would have killed me for what I saw there. They scan you for electronics before you enter so you won't record anything. They learned their lessons from the early part of the century. Too many of their kind were caught and blackmailed for their…proclivities. In turn, they became the best blackmailers so they could get away with their tastes."

Kevin offered my father and Russell a cigar each. I was shocked. My dad was totally clean. I'd seen him smoke only once, when my baby brother Richard was born. Russell, and Terry had cigars and fished from the lake on that day.

"When I first got into Hollywood, they wanted to take my daughter," Kevin reminisced. "I didn't do it. They were talking about how I'd get $25 million a picture, like the biggest stars. They took one of your kids and they'd run trains on your ass. That was the deal. Most actors became alcoholics to forget what they were doing."

"You won an Oscar right at the start," said Russell.

"It was good in the beginning. I would have won one or two more but it all went politically correct. I won the award and then they really came down on me. I hadn't given them my daughter. They wanted me in the CIA movies, the ones with the biggest budgets."

"The ones where they trained white people to hate themselves," observed my father. "The ones where they trained the races to mix with each other, just before the country broke apart."

"You said it, I didn't," said Kevin whimsically as he puffed from his cigar. "You couldn't even think those things in my industry. They'd sniff you out,"

"There were trials," I said. I remembered how an ex-President was hanged publicly for resisting the agenda but they painted him as a foreign agent. The fire crackled as Kevin put on another log. We only burned pine at home. Kevin had black walnut, flown in from somewhere. The wood burned so nicely.

"Where is your daughter?" Dale asked.

"She's with her mother in Iowa," Kevin answered. "We separated to keep her safe. Once I was away from them, they left us alone."

"And Milo?" my father asked.

"They didn't want boys then, just girls."

I was chilled hearing that, for some reason. I couldn't wrap my head around it and turned my attention back to the glass of water I had been nursing. My eyes were getting heavier by the dim light of the fireplace. I glanced over to see Dale eyeing the cigars on the coffee table at our feet.

"We saw them take a boy a couple years ago," my Dad started.

"Where?" Kevin asked.

"At the farmers market. They called him a 'draft dodger'. The boy was only 10 at the most. They were lying through their teeth. The parents gave in like it meant nothing. We saw the men with makeup and beards step out of black van. That's when we knew. The last time anyone put up a fight they put forty Somalis in a work camp up in St. Regis. Ran them through town just to scare everyone like they were there to stay permanently."

"How did I miss that?" Kevin asked. "The Federation outlawed that."

"Some good 'the Federation' did," my father mused. "Talk about a defunct government."

"Amen," said Kevin. "My sister raised her boys as girls and vice versa. Haven't talked to her for years. Last I talked to her she was trying to sell them. She wanted me to set her up with someone who would buy them. I couldn't say anything. You just have to shut up and move on. You did, anyway. Now, anything goes."

There was a long pause in the conversation.

"It's getting late," my father said as he stepped over Dale to bring me a blanket. "We've got a lot of riding ahead of us tomorrow."

Dale and I stayed out on the giant leather couches in the great room. Our fathers and Kevin went to their separate rooms. My last thoughts before I fell asleep were on the road ahead of us and what madness lay in wait wherever the satanic pedophiles lived. I couldn't believe we were going to hunt *them*. In my lifetime, the equation had only ever flowed in the other direction. Things had only ever fallen apart. The only news was truly terrible news. This was a chance at justice, at something going right in the world. I was ready to play my part.

There were more drones in the valley, searching for Kevin. Three of them, to be exact. We watched far away from a Western ridge through binoculars as they scoured Kevin Tedrick's property. There was nothing to worry about as Milo and his wife were far away already, heading south into Idaho to a remote cabin. Kevin muttered under his breath about what a fortune the drones must have cost. The drones couldn't be up in the sky for too long without burning through their fuel cells. In this fallen world bereft of power grids, a recharge would take days or longer. Sure enough, the drones blasted off back north in the direction we were heading.

The west side of the valley was rugged and pitched. We benefitted from a logging road that ran halfway up the valley before veering into it. That was as far as we made it the first day. Kevin was tired and his wounds weren't totally healed. He could walk around with just a hitch in his stride but he was asking Dale to fetch things for him. I liked seeing my buddy be useful to a man whose movies I adored. It was a surreal experience and I felt ever the spectator.

We would stay in the mountains and ignore the turn in the logging road. This was unhappy news for me as I was sore from the saddle. Being so young still, I wondered how I would keep up the next two days with these three sturdy men leading the way.

On the second day we stopped again to watch a drone zoom through the valley on the east side. There was a single truck driving on the highway. The drone hovered above the truck before going south in the direction of Kevin's place. A few errant rifle shots rang out from the truck but the drone was already out of range. My father commented on the obvious massive caliber of the weaponry those folks had. What reason they had for heading north, I hadn't the slightest, but I was envious of their zippy progress. Nobody was interested in them. We had to stay up in the mountains in the thick tree cover. The drones were ten feet across and couldn't fly in the forest. They were large enough to carry off whole persons.

That night Kevin produced a cell phone he'd kept in a lead box the past two years. It synched to a small speaker and we had quiet music to give us life after a long day's ride. It was the first music I had heard in almost a year. He kept the soundtracks to his movies on the phone, so most of it was instrumental. We used to all be so interconnected with the Internet. All the information and entertainment you could ever want right at your fingertips. Consciousness was different then. Your subconscious mind was always and forever chewing on competing narratives and the actions of a few brave souls facing down the mob. Now that space was empty. I hardly retained a knowledge of that emptiness anymore. I was glad for the relief of not having to care about far off figures anymore. I could tell this wasn't the case for my father. He spoke about it that night.

"You have to wonder which governments are faring the best," he said was we listened to the soft piano music. "The one in DC, the one in Chicago, the one in Seattle, the one in San Francisco…"

"There were a bunch of them there by the end," said Russell.

"Seattle was the only one that wasn't nuked to oblivion. Goddamn Chinese," my father said with a chuckle. "They were always ahead of the curve."

"But somehow Beijing and Shanghai got the worst of it," noted Kevin. He was rebandaging his leg and sitting back against a towering pine. He put a tube of gel back into his rifle bag and I caught a glimpse of his weapon. It was the same as the ones on my father and Russell's backs. I decided all three weapons belonged to Kevin. My concentration on the rifles broke when my father spoke again.

"I didn't know," said my father. "They were dealing as bad as they got, I'll say that. They finished off half of their continent."

"Deseret is fairing the best, their head families anyway," said Kevin. "They quarantined their zone before the fall. The families that had bunkers in western Wyoming and up through Park City came out after the EMP's and nukes. They had a vaccine for the plague."

"*Nobody* has those," said Russell. "Those are worth millions."

I knew there were plagues. We read bits and pieces about them when there was still some sovereign information on the Internet. Governments simply went around killing the people who made encrypted platforms, destroying their servers, and requiring all service providers to run state of the art blocking software. You had to infer things from what was presented to you. Sometimes presenters or journalists would go rogue and tell you what they knew before they'd get shut down.

"I've got a few vials," said Kevin. Both Russell and my father widened their eyes in surprise before leaning in to hear more. "A traveler broke into my cabins near Darby, at the edge of the ranch. When I trained the security system on to him, he gave them up. Had to shoot him in arm before he would budge. He had a few more on him but I wasn't there to frisk him."

"You were watching from your place," my father observed. "How do you know the vaccines are legit?"

"His kid had the plague. He had her with him. He only had the vials, no syringes. He put a few vials in a security box and then I let him know where to find the syringes he needed. Stupid son of a bitch was kind, I'll give him that. But he was stubborn. I made sure the bullet was superficial. I don't need that kind of karma on my conscience. I let him stay until she was recovered enough to move on. He was stubborn, wanted to stay. I turned up the air on him. It was 110 Fahrenheit in there before he took her and cleared out. That place is running on hydroelectric, so I had all the time in the world to sweat him out. He wasn't going to destroy anything because he knew I'd put a bullet in him if it got to that."

"What'd you learn from him?" my father asked. I could feel my curiosity about the wider world starting to come back. This traveler's story was sympathetic and deep in the back of my mind I hoped his daughter was my age so I could have a girlfriend.

"Most of it I already mentioned," Kevin replied. "He got the vials from a dying patriarch. The old bugger's family had defected from the Church. The only son was a homosexual and didn't want to hide it any longer. The old guy couldn't accept it and so the gay son, his wife – who was more a friend at that point, their two kids, and a 'best friend' headed out to Colorado to try and escape the Deseret patrol before the whole zone was closed off. Our traveler friend was a ranch hand at the old patriarch's place and took the vials as the man lay dying in bed. He headed north to find family before his daughter came down with it in Arco. He got as far as my place on a bike before she was too sick to continue. He said he was lucky he didn't get it because everyone in eastern Idaho was getting it. He said it comes in waves. You won't see it for a while and then it breaks out again."

"No wonder no one comes up through the pass," I said.

"A lot of people have gone south though… the plague is the worst part of it. Milo and Jen will be alright and that's good enough for me," Kevin said with a pained look.

"Anything else about down south?" Dale asked eagerly. He seemed to sense that Kevin was shutting down for the night and wanted to get what little he could out of him.

Kevin scratched at his beard and pondered the question before answering, "The water supply for the Salt Lake Valley was poisoned with bad stuff. The Elders didn't tell anyone but their families. They let it ride for weeks while whole cities died. The fall hit and this winter killed most of the rest off. The patriarch told the traveler that the Elders were the ones who poisoned the water. The rationale was that there wasn't enough food to go around anyway. It was a preemptive strike against looting and scavenging. The elite culled their herd. It worked for them, in a sense."

We all were quiet. The music was soothing but not enough to quiet my thoughts on what the Salt Lake story implied. These horrors were happening everywhere. Only the strongest and craftiest were surviving. The world had blown open into a full apocalypse. The thought exhausted me.

A drone flying down into the valley woke me on the third day. I could barely see it through the cloud cover.

We had made it much further in the night than I had realized. When I went to pee away from the camp, it surprised me to look down on the burnt-out waste that had been Missoula. There were houses in the hills, here and there, and a few buildings left standing near the university campus. I could see the crumbling dome of a mosque near the river. The streets were strewn with newer cars. I looked for the truck I had seen the day before but gave up when my father called to me. I picked my gun belt up from where I had set it and trudged up the hill back to camp.

Everyone was mounted and ready to go. The trail was a lot easier in this area. The steep path became more regular and gentler. I was happy for it as I was still sore. We would reach our destination in the afternoon. My anxiety was high. My father seemed to sense this as he looked back at me to give me a smile as if to say that it was going to be okay. I glanced at the drone strapped to Kevin's back and hoped that whatever it was going to do would be enough for everyone to make it out alive.

I thought about my sister Wendy. She would eventually go into the world to find a husband. I didn't want that for her. The ugliness of everything was setting in for me. There was a lot less peace and a lot more people dead than I realized. For as long as it was a consideration in our family, we thought Wendy would find someone in Missoula. We were untouched in our mountain home near Russell's family. There was play, study, and some hunting. I didn't think about killing. The concept had only come to me in the days previous. I knew Wendy could live with some of it but I didn't want for her to have to experience the sickness I felt in the pit of my stomach. She was so kind and attentive. How could she attend to all this death and pandemonium? I missed my sister and hoped I would see her again.

My dad had said many times when I was young that he hoped Missoula would one day burn to the ground. As the world fell apart, he said it less and less. It had been years since he last said it. I wondered what was going through his head as I looked down on the devastation. Nobody much liked Missoula but nobody I knew sincerely wanted to burn it to the ground. Apparently, some people did.

The wreckage passed out of sight as the trail once again veered to the west. I was relieved just enough to notice my anxiety for what was to come. The closer we were to Alberton, the more anxiety I felt.

"Petty Creek," said Kevin as we came down from a mountain path and approached a paved road. He held up his hand for us to stop. He and my father dismounted. They motioned for Dale and I to wait. Russell took the opportunity to put some chewing tobacco in his mouth. Kevin and my father walked cautiously into the clearing and crouched down. They muttered something between them and my father took his binoculars from his chest to look around. I could feel the danger in the area we were entering. They strode back to us when Kevin seemed satisfied. I could hear Russell spit on the ground.

"We dumped out onto the road closer than I thought," said Kevin. "We're two hours away, if we walk. They're in a ridge north of town. It's a glass building, if you'd believe it."

We heard a distant rumble to the south coming up the road. I followed the adults as they led us back up the slope where we'd be out of sight. The rumble was close now. It sounded like a bus or a truck. Kevin jumped down from his horse and ran low to a place he could see the road from. The rumble passed and I could tell whatever it was, it had a diesel engine.

"That was a school bus," Kevin said with a grimace. The physical effort was getting to him. "A fucking school bus."

The men were bewildered. We crossed to the west side of the road as quickly as possible and kept out of sight. We eventually came up over a ridge and looked down on the Clark Fork River. I could see rainbows painted on the rooftops of all the large buildings and some of the smaller houses with metal roofs. Dale stifled a laugh. We rolled our eyes at one another. I thought the town looked stupid.

Looking through his binoculars, my father said, "There's people at the school- a bunch of them. They have tables out. It's a barbecue."

None of us had anticipated there being people in town. It was just assumed that people from Missoula would overrun it and pick it clean. The gears in my head were turning, trying to make sense of the new information.

I saw my dad shift his gaze to the right. He said, "The highway and the bridge are blocked off."

I looked and could barely make out what he'd pointed out.

The men conferred and decided we would end around the town on the east side as there was far less activity there. I was shocked to see what looked like a functioning town when I looked through my father's binoculars. I surmised that these pedophile people had spared the town whatever had hit Missoula. They must be the patrons of the whole situation.

With some difficulty and a great care not to be seen by anyone, we crossed the river and rode swiftly to cover. We rode up a steep ridge and came into distant view of a large glass building ringed by hundreds of large solar panel arrays. I picked out the bright yellow of what looked like a school bus driving away from the place. My heart pounded in my chest.

"This is as far you boys go," said Kevin. "Jim, hold on to this."

He touched the screen of the phone with the music on it several times before handing it to me. From his pocket he produced what looked like a small antenna and a black electronic brick. He plugged both of them into the phone.

"Keep this in your pocket here," he said as he dropped the brick into my jacket lapel pocket. I could feel Dale peering over my shoulder in envy as his father loosely tied the horses up to trees in the vicinity. "And keep this antenna pointed at that glass building at all times. Take turns if you get tired."

I looked at the screen. It showed a satellite map of where we were and a dot relative to us where the glass building should have been. The satellite map was blocked out in black right on that spot.

"The passcode is 1-1-1-1, if the screen goes out on you," Kevin said to me with a wink. "That thing's worth a small fortune so don't let it out of your sight."

When I looked up from the phone, I saw Russell giving his son a goodbye hug. Dale was sniffling. We'd both been tough to this point. My legs weakened as my father put his hand on my shoulder. We embraced. I said to him, "Dad, they didn't do anything to *us*. They're probably helping those people in town."

"As innocent as they look, those rainbows stand for something terrible, Jim," he said.

I watched Kevin inject himself with something in his leg. He breathed a tremendous sigh of relief.

"I know," I said to my father.

"The school bus had Indian kids in it," Kevin called over to me. He was setting the drone on the ground and powering it up. The drone sprang to life and flitted silently up into the air. I was impressed as all the drones I'd ever seen were loud and obvious. Maybe they were that way for a reason. He watched his lithe drone for a moment and then turned back to his horse. He withdrew a belt full of grenades and strapped it around his chest.

I watched the men trudge down the slope, armed to the teeth. As the slope eased, they opened up into a trot. It was the second time in a week I had watched the most important people in my life head out, armed, into harm's way. There would be violence soon.

Dale pointed out to me that the drone app on the phone had camera options. I hesitated to leave the satellite view but went ahead and switched to the drone's view. We could see the glass building clearly from an angle. There were two guards checking on a security door that seemed to be malfunctioning. It opened and closed erratically. The crackle of rifle fire sounded out and both fell in a heap. There were no other guards in sight. Soon I saw my father come into view and check on the guards. I winced as he shot one twice in the center of his chest. Russell and Kevin came into view and all of them ducked in through the door, one by one, after propping it open.

"Your dad just killed somebody," gasped Dale. I was shocked but not numb. What I saw didn't confuse me or hurt me. I knew these were bad men who died.

Three Indian kids scrambled out of the building through the open security door. They clung to each other. I zoomed the camera in and for a moment I saw one of them clutching a pistol that looked like my father's. The kids scurried down the winding driveway. I looked away from the phone to see them with my own eyes before I lost them in the tree cover. I was relieved for them. They looked like hell. I noticed the path lights along the driveway were flickering erratically.

One of the large drones that belonged to the hideous people in the glass building roared into view above us. I was momentarily terrified before the rotors flipped instantly and the drone came crashing down at almost a ninety-degree angle. I could see it was still powered on though the rotors had powered down. There were red flashing lights along its side. Our drone had scrambled its system. One of the rotors turned on and with a booming clatter the drone smashing upside down into a tree before going back to its strange stasis.

Dale threw a rock at it and came short by twenty feet. He pointed at the phone to note I was no longer pointing it at the glass building. I resumed my duties and we continued to watch the scene unfold on the phone. Three loud thumps shook the building. The third one emitted a shockwave that shattered the entire south facing glass panel. More Indian children spilled out of the security door. To my overwhelming relief, my father came back into view. He had his rifle trained on the perimeter of the building and was walking diligently around the massive patio. He was looking for any remaining guards. Russell stepped out into view through the broken edifice. One of the Indian kids that straggled behind the others on the way down the driveway turned back and clamored to Russell. He gesticulated toward the driveway and the boy refused. Russell shrugged and the boy hung around. He looked about my age. It was hard to tell. Kevin was the last to emerge from the building. He was dragging what looked like a slender woman tied up by her hands and feet. He kicked her in the ribs and swore loudly enough that we could hear him all the way up at our vantage point. He spoke into his wristwatch. His voice came through on the phone, telling Dale to bring a horse. Dale was quick to do as he was told.

I watched them load the woman on the back of the pack horse. They all came up to where I was, including the Indian boy. I could see it wasn't quite a woman on the horse. It looked like a woman that had once been a man. Its mouth was gagged and makeup run down the face. It wore a strange pendant on its neck that now hung down on its face. I curled my lip in disgust as Kevin took the gear from me and recalled his drone back to where we were.

Dale said to me matter-of-factly, "He's our prisoner."

"Why didn't they kill him?" I asked.

"There's one more of them in town right now."

Two large explosions in quick succession blew open the underbelly of the glass building. The building groaned and partially collapsed in on itself. I watched Kevin withdraw a chipset from the drone that was crashed a short distance away. It died completely but not before he put three .45 rounds into it.

"That's it for their tech," he said as he menacingly shoved the chipset into the face of our prisoner. The man whimpered. I imagined they knew something I didn't. Kevin holstered his pistol and wrapped his prize in a bandana before putting it into his vest pocket.

I looked at the Indian boy and for the first time noticed he was in his underwear. He was sitting on his knees and staring at the ground. Dale took his spare shirt from his pack and gave it to the boy. He dressed himself. The shirt was too big but he looked relieved to have it on. I remembered a pair of swimming trunks I'd packed on the naïve chance we'd do some swimming. I brought him the trunks and he put them on. "Are you hurt?" I asked.

"They didn't do it to me yet. They make me watch," he said in a low voice.

I glanced at the prisoner and back at him. All I felt was disgust.

"What's your name?" asked Dale.

"Chogan."

Once everything was set to go, the men conferred in hushed voices. Dale gave Chogan a stick of jerky while we waited on them to decide whatever it was that they were deciding. Chogan ate greedily and scratched at the soles of his bare feet. I looked up into the air over and over, wondering if there'd be another drone. The suspense was killing me and so I blurted out to my father, "Dad, are there more drones coming?"

"No, son," he called back. "We blew them up."

They came to a consensus. My father patted Kevin on the shoulder, which surprised me. Russell and Kevin mounted up and rode down to the glass building. "They're grabbing a few things," said my father.

"Where'd those other kids go?" I asked.

"There's a Christian camp not far from here. The pastor there knows most of them. They said he's safe."

"What about Chogan?"

"Who?"

I pointed to the boy.

"He wants to tell the townspeople what happened here," said my father.

"We're going into town?" I asked.

There was a small parade when we got into town. We had a clear vantage point from the ride down into town and the men picked out the largest float at the center of the procession. There on a throne sat another person who looked like our prisoner only this one was wearing a fake goatee and goat horns on its head. The strangest part of the sight was a burly man wearing leather straps and not much else with a pistol strapped to his hip. He was dancing sensually as the people had their children run up to the float and place money at his feet. Most of them did so only begrudgingly, like a spell was over them.

I followed the adults, with Chogan riding with me as we bounded out from a side street directly into the path of the float. Kevin and Russell had pistols trained on the dancer while my dad had the rifle I watched him kill a man with, at the ready. He eyed the small crowd but no one was making a move. The townspeople down the block from either direction plodded slowly to within earshot as if they were zombies. A few of the livelier ones were clearly in awe of our movie star leader.

Kevin bellowed, "These two have been hurting your children."

I scanned the small crowd and saw not a single Indian. Nobody was in the least bit surprised.

Kevin spun his horse around for effect. He came right up to the float and pointed his pistol right in the face of the dancer. "Drop it," he growled. The man complied.

"Mr. Tedrick," an older man called as he emerged into the street. "Welcome to our town." He walked out beside the float, holding out his hand. He was a kindly look man with white hair and a western suit jacket on that distinguished him from most of the other people. He and Kevin shook hands and the man introduced himself as Erick Carlsen. He had once been the sheriff of this town. Before we knew what was happening, the man drew a Colt from under his armpit and shot the dancer straight through the heart. He fired one more shot into the man's ribs as he lay bleeding, stone dead on the float.

There was sporadic clapping among the beleaguered people. Erick drew a bead on the woman thing on the throne before it yelled, "Wait!"

"Go on then," said Erick.

"We'll release the plague into town!" the enthroned person screeched.

Erick looked flummoxed and wavered.

"We have nearly a hundred vials of antivirals here. We took them from their vault," said Kevin.

That seemed to satisfy Erick and he fired the fatal shot through the person's forehead just as it was screaming, "No!"

Erick then walked over to our prisoner and executed him with a shot through the back of the head. There was more applause from the crowd but this time with renewed spirit indicating our prisoner was the worst perpetrator of the lot. I was shocked at the suddenness of the killings but not at their brutality. My father helped Erick untie the body from the horse and they dragged it over to the front porch of the feed and supply store. A number of men from the gathered crowd came and took the dancer and the devil woman from the float and propped them up next to our prisoner. A fiddle was produced and a true festive spirit gripped the small town.

Chogan and I hopped off our horse. He smiled widely as a woman came up to us with glass jars full of lemonade to drink. It tasted like the powder kind. My mouth puckered and a big grin came over my face.

The bodies were left behind at the feed-and-supply and everyone made their way over to the school where there had been a small contingent of people cooking for the benefit of everyone else. I noticed there weren't many children around. The women held back while Kevin conferred with the important men of the town. Lots of questions were being put back and forth, much like when we had first come to know Kevin. I edged closer to the conversation, as far as there was room in the crowd for the horse I led by hand.

"We blew the two up down in the valley, two more at their complex and one I shot to pieces," Kevin said loudly.

"You shot it down with that?" Erick asked, pointing his thumb at the drone on Kevin's back.

"No, no. This knocked it out of the sky," he patted the drone over his shoulder, "-and this," he patted his pistol, "blew the thing to pieces. Their drones were shit. All bark, no bite."

A relieved murmur echoed through the men walking around Kevin and Erick. My father and Russell were up ahead already, tethering their horses and having plates of food thrust upon them.

"At first we thought they were good. Strange, but good," said Horace, a towering blonde man with bushy eyebrows. I was seated at the table of honor along with Mr. Carlsen, the men of our group, Dale, and three other town patriarchs, one of them an elderly man.

"They brought the power back on after the fall," the elderly man chimed in. "We had to paint our roofs in exchange."

"They kept a lot of people alive with their food stores and medicines. But always the drones were," said Horace as he pointed into the sky and raised his bushy eyebrows.

"Then they wanted their pageants," said Erick. "In the dead middle of winter, too. 'Give us our pageant or we'll shut the power down'."

"We gave them their pageant at the school. They wanted story time with our children the next week. Said they had movie cameras and they did. They had their 'renewal techs' set up a whole elaborate filming."

"You didn't try to get help," my father asked.

"There's one satellite uplink that comes through, for two hours a night," said Erick. "They figured out how to jam the signal. Their renewal techs did it for them."

Erick saw the confused looks on all our faces but Kevin's and explained, "Near as we figure it, they brought those big gay men into their cult in the past two years. That's when we started seeing them around town. The 'renewal techs' kept the machinery going while those pricks did their sick thing."

Horace added, "We didn't *really* understand what was going on until a week ago. Did you see the blockade to the east? We put that up. They poisoned everyone in Huson with the plague. Maybe a couple dozen people who stayed through winter. But some of them tried to come through. It was nasty."

"They said they'd do the same to us if we didn't comply."

"The children," Kevin noted sourly.

"They were after the children," said Erick. "We outnumbered them but their drones were worth a hundred men each when you don't have the tech to take them down."

"They raped a kid just over there, in front of everyone," said Horace. "There's an orphanage south of here. They kept the kids alive through the winter, grooming them the whole time. When we wouldn't give up our kids, they made their public display. Five drones circling our town with all their techs armed and at the ready. A couple of us went out for help but there's nobody east or west of here. We were going to send people south tonight, but you know the rest."

"There's more of these satanics," said Kevin. "None that I know of in Montana but there's an outfit in Sun Valley. If these drones fueled up anywhere outside of here, we'll know when we get back to my place." He produced the chip he had taken from the drone he'd destroyed.

"Guess we got to put together a hunting party. You got any more of those rifles at your place?" Erick asked as he motioned to the weapons still on Russell and my father's backs.

"Oh yeah. Got nearly a dozen more. We can go hunting, no problem."

Two groups of men went up to the glass compound to scavenge what they could. My father went with them. I waited in town with Dale. Chogan was gone. Some women had taken him in. A lawyer fellow went with them and was asking him questions. I was skeptical of what good it would do as clearly there was no law in the land. Dale and I took to playing with some other boys at the school playground. It was fun to be around kids our own age, but I felt apart from them. This journey I'd been on changed my perspective. The image of my father killing someone kept ringing in my head, like there was something I was supposed to learn from it. Later I would learn there was a lesson there about the hardness of the tooth and nail world we lived in, but this was my last expedition with my father for a few years. There came to be a whole network of courageous men, with Kevin Tedrick and a much younger man the epicenter, who gladly took up the roles Dale and I had played. We got to be kids.

We stayed the night in Alberton and the next morning a dozen men, including Erick and Horace, joined us on the trail back to Kevin's base of operations, Big Country Ranch. These twelve men represented perhaps a third of the town's able-bodied men. They said their goodbyes to their women, children, and friends. We rode out of town and crossed on the bridge south that had been cleared of its blockade. Chogan whistled loudly to me from the town side of the bridge just as our procession was clearing it. He smiled widely and waved happily, bouncing forward on his toes. I could see he had on clothes that fit him well. I waved back. In my heart I wished him the best.

The ride back down into the valley was much quicker than the ride up. We took the main roads and though they hadn't been repaved in years, they weren't in too bad of shape. I still couldn't believe how few people were out and about in the valley. We were easily the largest group we encountered the entire way. I surprised to see one of those casino bar and grills open on the highway that ran the length of the valley. We lunched there and found out from the shrewd owner that he had buried several tons of materials and electronic equipment deep underground in storage tanks as a precaution. He envisioned running his place in just the kind of world we found ourselves in. He was imaginative and trusting, especially when he heard what we'd done about the drones and the people controlling them. He treated our entire troop to a tasty mead he'd made himself, when he learned what the mission had been. We paid him in a few boxes of ammunition upon leaving. That and working electronics were the new currency.

Dale and I and our fathers split off from the group to go home. Our fathers would rejoin the rest of the men the next day on their ride into Idaho. They hoped it would be a straight shot they could get done in a week and the rumors of plague down there were assuaged by the newfound presence of the vials that carried the cure. Kevin sent us away with enough for our families, a sight my mother would surely be relieved to see.

We entered the part of the valley I was most familiar with and all the tension left my body. Up the winding road to our place we went. My sister Wendy was with my mother, pruning fruit trees in the fenced orchard at the front of the property. She called out with joy and ran to my father, who dismounted and took her up in his arms. I gave my mother a tremendous hug. I laughed as I watched my little brother scamper out of a tree to go poke at one of the weapons strapped on the side of Russell's horse. Spring was in full bloom at this altitude.

That night I slept like a baby.

Part Two

A warning shot rang out from Sutton's cabin. The bullet zipped by him like an angry hornet and ricocheted on the rocky outcropping behind him. His horse was spooked and reared up. He pulled her lead rope with him as he sprang back and out of view of the cabin. He cursed and spit in a rage from cover. A squatter had taken over his cabin. The distinct hum of a four-wheeler engine coming to life spurred him on his horse and he took off at a gallop. He wasn't taking any chances on tenants as unfriendly as these. That was his friend's four-wheeler. That was his cabin. He spit again.

That night he returned to peer down at the cabin from the rocky outcropping. He crawled into sight and looked down into the bay window of the cabin at a distance of a hundred yards. He could see three figures, two of them men. The third was unclear to him. They were eating his food, burning his firewood, and wasting his kerosene to light up the place like decadent idiots. Sutton cursed and spit.

The click of a hammer cocked back froze him dead on the ground. He took a shallow breath, expecting to be blown away.

"Sutton?" the voice asked.

"Greg?" he replied.

The danger had passed. Sutton relaxed and Greg helped him to his feet.

"Glad to see you," Greg exclaimed, trying not to raise his voice with the elation he felt.

"Should we try for it? They're real jumpy."

"It'll be a dogfight. We should try for it," said Greg.

The unmistakable grinding of dirt bikes roared up from the county road some distance away. Sutton and Greg hurriedly took their horses further away from the private road to the cabin where they knew the horses wouldn't be spotted. They returned to their vantage point. It was a half moon, enough to see the squatters drunkenly amble out to greet the rest of their gang: four men and three women dressed in camo fatigues.

"Goddamnit, if we only had the guys with us…" Greg growled like a cougar. His voice was full of hatred for the bandits he saw before them. Back in the city they had two other friends who had put money into helping Sutton build his place up and stock it with supplies. Before the quarantine was back in effect, they had kept a steady rotation in their friend group, always manning the place with one or two guys.

"They didn't make it out."

"Didn't think they did. It was George Rodgers."

"It was George," confirmed Greg. "Who else would it be?"

They were referring to a nationalist political meeting their two other friends had attended six months prior. Their contact had been a man named George Rodgers, the first political contact anyone in the friend group had had in the time since they had taken their contracts in Western Oregon. George Rodgers turned out to be an agent of the Matriarchy and in the days before power to the city went down, his face had been on every billboard owned by the Party. He was their next supposed candidate for a city council position, the candidacy being a mere overture as everyone knew the Party's control of the city was complete. If they matriarchs wanted a front man to cool political resentments, they would do it. Only the lure of high paying, lavish employment had kept the friends rooted to the city. Their heterosexuality, avoidance of narcotics, and several other indicators that marked them as the enemy to the prevailing culture had been tolerated on account of their contract status. Now the bandits in the cabin were set for years to come on the back of so much sacrifice and risk. The bandits had appeared to overcome the security measures that guarded their fuel supplies, a technical proficiency that surprised Greg and Sutton – given the boorish behavior they displayed.

"Let's check the Hobbit Hole," suggested Sutton, referring to a small backup hovel on the other side of the 20-acre property they had only broken ground on in the last months. The swing of a flashlight in someone's hand at a short distance, obviously on a nighttime patrol of the grounds, spurred the two men along.

The property had been chosen for its thick timber cover and relative distance to Timothy Lake, a beautiful and relatively untouched mountain lake overlooked by Mt. Hood.

The Hobbit Hole was stocked just as they had left it two weeks prior. There were water bricks, light caliber weapons and ammunition, foodstuffs, and an assortment of other essentials for anyone eyeing a long winter in the mountains. The Hole itself was a poured concrete bunker framed by rebar with the rudiments of an air exchange sticking out of the top, work only having been started in the last two visits to the spot. The cabin had seen most of the work. This was a brief project spawned by paranoia and the fact that air patrols, both Chinese and Matriarchy, had begun to prevent travel out of Western Oregon in the past two months. The fact that the last leave had been given only on the stipulation that no one could leave east of the Cascades or north of the Columbia was enough to switch on a survival gear in the original four friends.

"We can't stay here," said Sutton. "They shot at me on sight."

"They're real jumpy," Greg repeated from earlier.

"Where'd you get your horse, by the way?"

"Off a dead guy. I was going to ask you the same thing."

"There was a farm burning down on 26. There was no gas on the way out here so I switched over. I didn't think you knew how to ride."

"Just a bit," Greg laughed.

They took what they needed to make the trip west back to Portland to try and find their friends. They agreed going on horseback made the most sense as the Western Oregon government had suddenly cut off gasoline supplies in the region. There were rumors the power grid would go down soon, as had already happened in many other places around the globe. The entrance to the Hobbit Hole was covered over with brush. Any person passing by would have to look closely to realize what was there. The men hoped the cache would remain untouched in case they needed to return. They rode through the night and slept on the side of a road just as day broke.

In the afternoon, a family in a red passenger van passed them going the other direction before honking and reversing. The friends were surprised to see a full, intact family together as such relations were outlawed. It had been months since either had seen a full family as nobody risked open visitations in public.

"You guys are crazy if you're going back to the city," said the father of the family. He had on spectacles and bore a wispy beard on his face, which was a more common sight on women.

"Shouldn't you be wearing makeup?" Sutton asked jokingly.

"Shouldn't you?" was the immediate retort.

The man smiled and introduced himself as Paul. He gave a strange handshake and seemed puzzled when Sutton and Greg did not reciprocate. He gave the names of his wife and two children and said they were going to their home in a commune in central Idaho. He asked the two friends, "Don't you know about the quarantine?"

"We slipped it," replied Greg.

"On those?" said Paul, motioning to the horses.

"Believe it or not."

A sedan came into view on the country road, loaded on top with cans of gasoline and boxes ratcheted down on the roof. The deeply tinted driver's window rolled down and a hand emerged to wave as the sedan approach. Paul pulled his family's van to the side of the road and the sedan pulled up alongside.

"Headed over the pass?" asked the driver. He was a short, stocky man wearing a flannel shirt. His face was modified with prosthetic bumps and a portion of the bridge of his nose was gone. A slender woman nervously chewed her fingernails in the front seat. She had a small dog in her lap.

"Oh yeah, getting away from the madness," Paul noted. The man was surprised at the forthrightness of this 'micro-aggression'. Commenting on the mental health of another person or place in a way that could be construed as negative was strictly forbidden by the Western Oregon Legislature and generally brought prison time. ·

The driver and his woman in the front seat were at a loss for words. The man was troubled. He raised his hands in defeat and gave a small wave before continuing his drive eastward. Sutton considered that this man was likely the kind of person to turn others in for hate speech.

"Maybe I shouldn't have said it that way," said Paul.

"Fuck him," said Sutton. "He saw we were unmarked. That's why."

"The Chinese want the city," Paul said of Portland. "A little bird told me Liu Zhao is holding President Brown hostage. He's got a small army in the congressional building and another at the nuclear center on the east side."

"Some good the quarantine is doing. I thought Asian immigration was 'our cause to celebrate'. Some good it ever did. Too little, too late," said Greg.

"The kicker is that they're sweeping up all the separatists. They're not even stopping the enemy that has them by the…" Paul hesitated and looked at his wife before finishing, "-balls." He acted like a man starved for male company. He had been cooped up with gossipy women for too many years.

"The Chinese don't look kindly on gay rights anymore."

"The Vice President is at the nuclear center downtown. Says she'll destabilize the reactor and ruin the whole urban zone unless her wife is released," Paul alluded to the homosexual relationship between the President and Vice President. Only lesbian pairs had been elected to office in the past three election cycles, each pair more Communist than the previous. "Unless she's bluffing, a lot of people are going to die. The Chinese never back down."

"The United States isn't going to help?" Sutton referred to the small collection of US states in the Midwest that had split off and formed a European ethnocentric nation during the great Balkanization of the 51 states, including Puerto Rico.

"Hell no, they wouldn't help," Greg said to his friend. Greg took a cigarette from his shirt pocket and lit it.

"Where'd you get that?" asked Paul.

"Same place I got the horse."

Only narcotics and psychedelics were permitted in Western Oregon. Alcohol was permitted but only at County Fairs, which were essentially open-air orgies run by the state. Cigarettes were a symbol of a bygone masculine era and so possession by men, especially white men, could result in sterilization.

"Suits you," Sutton said to his friend.

The men laughed together before each remembered that raised voices among more than two men at a time was not permitted. The shared recognition of the warped culture they'd come from was cause for renewed laughter. Paul's wife smiled at the revelry of the men. Sutton brought on an uproar in the other men by listing several racial and sexually derogatory epithets in a row.

When the laughter subsided, Paul again ventured his original thread of inquiry. "You guys have to be crazy to go back there."

"Our buddies are back there," volunteered Greg with a hearty exhale of cigarette smoke.

"I understand. Why not go to Madras and try to get them visas?" Paul referred to the somewhat close Warm Springs Nation, which treated white men fairly well. A lot of men in Portland had made it back to the United States thanks to the Indian nation system. It was like a reverse Underground Railroad.

"We think they got found out for being nationalists."

Paul winced sympathetically. "The nationalists never had a chance. They haven't for 20 years. It's foolishness. You get in, make your money, and get out to whoever the hell will take you." He was referring to the small contingent of straight, white males who were kept in the city as breeding stock for the mixed-race matriarchy that prized them. The nationalist movement had originated in this small population and spread to some Hispanic and black zones before being rooted out and quashed by agents of the state.

"You were a breeder, too?" asked Sutton.

"Yup, she was my handler," Paul referred to his wife. "Those are pure kids in the backseat. She faked all the labs."

Sutton whistled loudly and Greg leaned forward to get a better look at the two children strapped to car seats in the back. Every free-born white child in Western Oregon was subject to hormonal therapy in-utero and body modification surgeries by age two. This was to treat their white privilege.

"No way *you're* going back," Sutton observed.

The men went quiet as a swarm of massive drones flew west toward the city of Portland. The swarm was flying low in a way that was menacing, their grappling arms clearly visible. These were crowd control drones dispatched from some unknown place to combat the coup d'état taking place.

"Never seen them fly in from that direction," said Sutton.

"Maybe *you're* not going back," said Paul.

"We are."

"Do you have a number?" the driver asked as he produced a cell phone.

Sutton and Greg looked at each other and shook their heads at the middle-aged man. Paul prompted his wife for a pen and pad. He wrote down the address of a place in central Idaho where the men would find provisions should they ever pass through that way. He drew in a map on the same paper and added that there would be the chance that he and his family would be at the cabin. He pricked his thumb with a ring on his hand, stamping his blood onto the paper. The other two men hid their discomfort.

A motorcycle roared into view, flying at an incredible speed. The horses were spooked but steadied by their riders. Atop the motorcycle was an Equality Officer. The officer was a woman with long, multicolored hair flying out from her helmet and face tattoos visible beneath her sunglasses. Her uniform was a mauve pantsuit with puffed shoulders. The men watched her as she approached, each tense with a thought to shoot her if she tried to detain them. A month prior, none of them would have thought to do so but it was obvious law and order had broken down completely in the past week. They were relieved as the Equality Officer picked up speed and roared past them.

"Where the hell could she be going?" asked Sutton.

"Hopefully not the way we're going," said Paul.

"We'll leave you to it."

The men shook hands and were on their separate ways.

Greg and Sutton rode for hours, all the while encountering more and more refugees streaming out of the Willamette Valley. Few of them rode horses. Most were overcrowded into electric vehicles that would soon run out of charge, some had classic gasoline vehicles, and the rest were on scooters. Not many people overtook Greg and Sutton going into the Valley. They disregarded the obvious danger, agreeing among themselves that they would leave once they knew what had happened to their friends. The town of Estacada came and went. By nightfall they were in Damascus. The roads were flooded with people and they found it difficult to continue going into the city as there was little room to maneuver. The wealthiest inhabitants of the city, all women, fled the city in their flying vehicles. There were ten in total, as Sutton counted. The moonless night was upon the riders. Another swarm of drones, smaller in size, swept across the sky and besieged a flying vehicle, downing it in a fireball that that made the refugees heading east gasp in agony. Greg felt annoyed at hearing so many female voices protesting the death of one of their elites; clearly, they had no idea who oppressed them into the obscene tax and social schemes of Western Oregon. Sutton was oblivious. The men veered from the highway and took a city road, with a few detours, they knew would take eventually them to the edge of the quarantine.

Their timing was prescient. A swarm of prison drones bore down on the flood of refugees, their green lasers scanning the implant chips of the mostly female crush of vehicles. Their targets were found. The drones alighted upon dozens of vehicles, sliced open their tops with red and orange lasers, and tentacles sprang from their undersides to rip the women away into the sky. Their screams were drowned out by the crunch of cars piling up and screaming figures exiting vehicles to go on foot. A boom echoed out from an armored vehicle with a mounted cannon firing at a cluster of drones that exploded into flames. The armored vehicle tore through bodies and crumpled vehicles beneath its elevated tracks as it sped into the city.

"This is no hostage situation," Sutton said to his companion as they watched the carnage roll out beneath them several hundred feet away. "They're making war on each other now."

"Let's pick it up," said Greg.

They spurred their tired horses from a gentle trot to a gallop. They carried on this way for the better part of an hour, winding through city streets Greg knew from his time at one of the birthing centers nearby. Row upon row of townhomes and condominiums spewed out women in the thousands and to their surprise, men in the hundreds. They were accustomed to seeing non-white men but the sudden appearance of white men such as themselves had them both rethinking their notions of the Matriarchy's absolute rule over Western Oregon. The electricity went down and panic turned to terror as people with short range vehicles were left with little recourse for leaving the city. Prized possessions were being packed into vehicles, such as huge televisions, sex toys, and drag parade outfits. The electricity came back on and then flickered from brownouts every few minutes. Nobody bothered the two riders. They were ghosts riding into oblivion.

Late into the night they approached the northern edge of Happy Valley and looked down a large hill onto the quarantine. The network of fences, guard towers, and vehicle checkpoints were originally built to contain an outbreak of a sexually transmitted disease colloquially termed Clown's that had gone airborne. Since the disease outbreak had been pacified, the quarantine had also been used to keep Asian migration out of the Portland Metro area, and finally to keep citizens in the Metro as a political gambit on the part of the Matriarchy.

Their horses would go no further. The men grazed them in the National Cemetery and slept in shifts until morning broke. A black man came within a hundred feet of them as they ate their breakfast, intent on stealing one of their horses. They spotted him as he appeared from behind a tree and fired their pistols at him. He fled, firing a small revolver behind him, one of the shots whizzing just past Greg's ear. They cursed the man loudly, mounted as quickly as they could, and continued into the innards of the city.

They were stunned to discover no moving vehicles and no drones in the sky as their environment became more and more urban. No electric services were running. Sporadic gunfire at a distance and the ever-present movement of people going in the opposite direction were their constant companions. They came close to the quarantine fencing to see that no Equality Officers were stationed there. Cautiously they inched their horses around the barrier arms of the vehicle checkpoints.

A short haired woman who had the facial tattoos of an Equality Officer but the clothes of a regular citizen peaked out from a toll booth and said to the two men, "You two are better off heading the other direction. The city isn't safe anymore."

"Why?" asked Greg.

"The Chinese are in control of everything."

She gasped in horror and they looked in the direction she was facing. A tremendous mushroom cloud formed over the heart of the city, still a fair distance away.

"Take me with you!" she shouted and stumbled out from the booth. They refused her and rode back through the quarantine and out the way they came. The soundwave of the nuclear explosion hit them just as the sky turned bright again and another mushroom cloud formed.

"There's no saving them," said Shroud. "We need to get the hell out of here."

Their ammunition served them well as the journey out of the Willamette Valley was much more dangerous. Nobody had access to a working vehicle. Horses were a rare commodity that close into the city. They rode through yards, over road barriers, and made mad dashes across what bridges they had to as the horde of refugees only grew in size. Many potshots were taken at the pair. Sutton was grazed by a bullet. Greg was pulled from his horse at one point. They rode hard. A third and fourth shockwave hit them in quick succession, and they looked back to see the originating mushroom clouds before pressing onward. The day was bloody. Their escape was miraculous and not without several deaths from their gunfire. They rode the rest of the day with guns drawn, pointing them at any crowd of walking refugees they passed.

As they strode into the tall pines of the Mt. Hood National Forest, Greg said to Sutton, "Back where we started."

"Indeed."

"Back to the Hobbit Hole?"

"There and then we'll head into Idaho and meet up with Paul. Let's rest a day."

"Catch a flight out of there?"

"Whatever hit here and shut everything down probably hit there, too. That's what happened in Eastern Europe, it spread out everywhere. There's no flights out of Idaho. The Federation is going to shit."

"Warm Lake then."

"Warm Lake."

They set up camp by the Clackamas river on the other side of the highway running in unison with the water. They tended to their superficial wounds and counted themselves lucky.

Sutton ran his hand through his ruddy brown hair to calm himself and thought of his friends back in Portland. Surely, they were dead. They had joined the same breeder cohort two years prior. They were recruited for their superb physical, reproductive, and intellectual capabilities by the Matriarchy. Some 'legacy' breeders had been selected from within Western Oregon's pool of men. They were grandfathered-in to permanent positions when the child enhancement laws came into place: laws that required the hormonal and surgical ruination of all white males born in Western Oregon. Paul was probably a legacy breeder. Sutton and Greg were originally from western Nebraska where "the men still ran things", as was the popular saying. Their fallen friends were together from the same professional handball team in northern Washington and had taken the breeder gig as a way of escaping the crumbling economy the Chinese had fabricated.

Sutton's family had run an orange farm using thermal heat in the severe Nebraska winters. He'd designed the system of cultivation himself when he was still a boy after his father's similar attempts had fallen short. As the youngest of three brothers, Sutton's birth had timed well with the slow trickle proliferation of genetic enhancement designer drugs administered in utero. He was taller, more intelligent, and more decisive than his brothers. The difference wasn't as significant as the doctors had promised. The scientific knowledge in the more than 20 years since had not advanced as hoped. The prominent geneticists of his society had hit a roadblock. Yet the performative advantage of the Reformed United States was undeniable. They led the continent in every conceivable economic and wellness metric. They were also the envy of the rest of the continent and subject to embargo by the rest as they were not ideologically aligned. In this uncertain climate endeavors such as tropical fruit cultivation and fish farming had become far more lucrative.

Sutton had left for Western Oregon more out of rebellion than anything else. He came from quiet, mostly neglectful parents. The allure of the breeder recruitment campaign promised a lifestyle that appealed to his youthful, vitalistic sensibilities. All of it proved to be true. He'd considered himself wise to have sent a good chunk of his earnings home, which his family reinvested in their enterprise. He now wondered what their status could be. If any lesson could be garnered from the previous decades of world events it was that nuclear detonations spread far and wide destroyed political alliances and brought great danger to the common man. There were no reliable national alliances since the balkanization of the original United States.

Life as a breeder featured the part time presence of a 'milking' machine to which he was attached several times a day, half of the week. He was pumped for semen and his semen was pitted against that of others in what was commonly referred to as 'races'. The Matriarchy was maintained through in vitro fertilization, though some women held on to their 'legacy' breeders. The clinical half of the breeder's week was offset by a half week of activities meant to offset the maladaptive psychological effects that had reared their heads in previous iterations of the breeder program. Both Sutton and Greg had found the refreshing portion of their week to be garish by the end and had thus been the most committed to building a redoubt when air travel was severely restricted.

Sutton reminisced about the second half of his weeks now. Breeders were fed the finest meals, consisting of superfoods meant to keep up their seminal quality for the duration of their three-year contracts. They were given free access to the most beautiful, unmarked but sterile women from within the upper echelons of the Matriarchy. All manner of opulent travel, VIP access to sporting events (which Sutton found boring because only women were allowed to participate in professional sports), and adventuring opportunities were given to the breeders. Breeders were in a select population of Western Oregon that did not have to obey traffic laws or mind Equality Officers, so long as they were in the second half of their week. Small discrepancies had begun to arise in the previous months as the Matriarchy came under more and more pressure to turn over their small country to the budding Chinese overclass that had developed in the wake of eased work restrictions. The Matriarchy's choice to quarantine the Portland Metro area had only exacerbated relations and led to austerity measures, including an end to free travel and event access for breeders. This jolt had pushed Sutton and his friends out of their playboy stupor and into the paranoia that saw two of them invest in nationalist politics and two of them invest in a hidden redoubt where air patrols were the lightest.

Sutton hungered for the rich seafood meals that had been so abundant just recently. The trail food in their packs was dry and salty. He shook the thought out of his mind as he remembered a conversation he and his friends had entered into when their contracts as breeders had lost their allure. They were sitting alone on a yacht in Youngs Bay outside of Astoria on a beautiful sunny day. It was their last days of boating privileges until further notice.

"This is boring," said Pietro, a tall, handsome Italian striker who hailed from Seattle.

"Bored? You of all people?" exclaimed Greg.

"Yes, I know. It's boring! We can have all the fun we want but they don't let us go home. I want to get fat. I want to drink. I want to fight someone. All of this is boring. The money's not good enough anymore. Look at this shit," Pietro shouted as he picked up a tray of expensive hors d'oeuvres and threw them to the deck. Immediately a machine darted out from the base of their table, navigated between their legs, and set to work cleaning the mess. Pietro grabbed the cleaning machine, it beeped anxiously, and he smashed it on the ship's railing before flinging it out into the water.

"We met with the nationalists," said Liam, a man much of the mold the Matriarchy preferred: tall, high cheekbones, and intelligent. He had been the goalkeeper on the team he and Pietro played for before their breeder contracts. "They're cutting a deal for Tillamook County and access to the coast with the Chinese if they give turn over one of the nuclear centers when they take over. They have women on the inside that will do it."

"That's bullshit," said Greg.

"No, it's true. I know one of them," said Liam.

"Not that part. It's bullshit that you met up with them. They're leaky. Haven't you seen the trials?"

"Easy for you to say," Pietro spouted. "We have to go back to Seattle in a year. Your country isn't giving out visas. We're fucked."

"You shouldn't have met with them," said Sutton. He was dressed in red swim trunks and a straw cowboy hat, which was contraband.

"Turn it up, will you?" Greg indicated to Liam to turn up the white noise they had playing on the bridge where the only listening device on the ship persisted. It was hardwired to the navigation and could not be disabled without attracting negative attention. Liam turned up the device emitting the white noise.

"We *did* meet with them," said Pietro. "Look, it floats." He pointed to the cleaning machine and laughed. "Sutton, why are you looking at me like that? Come on, it's funny."

"Did you mention our group?" the stern leader asked.

"Never."

"Shouldn't have done it," Greg repeated Sutton's admonishment. "We're trying to finish out our contracts and get out of here."

"They withheld our last paycheck," said Liam. "What makes you think they'll honor our contracts? The city's falling apart."

"If those racist bitches would just let some of those Chinese bastards fuck them!" yelled Pietro. "They just need a good fucking. They're too uptight. They're going to throw everything away because they're too *repressed*." Pietro was making light of the prevailing culture of free sex, public orgies, and female adult-child relationships.

Sutton wasn't in a joking mood. He pinched his lower lip between his thumb and index finger as he stewed over this latest development. Pietro calmed down and sat back down on the bench seating. Liam lit a cigar, which was also contraband.

"That cabin of ours," Sutton began.

A minute passed before he spoke again. Greg became contemplative like his best friend and set down his plate of food. He listened as Sutton laid out the plan they were to follow to save themselves were their host country to fall. There was little disagreement on the plan once it was promised to Pietro that their redoubt would be stocked with whatever weapons they could attain by corrupting their elevated roles in the society. Truth was, guns weren't so difficult to obtain anymore as the Chinese had flooded them onto the black markets in the Willamette Valley, despite a rigorous embargo from the Matriarchy.

Now on the Willamette River, Greg sat down next to his friend lost in thought. The day had mostly passed by and soon they would start a fire and have dinner. Greg produced another cigarette from its pack.

"Burning through those, huh?" Sutton noted.

"Why not? I won't smoke them again. May as well have some fun. You want one?" Greg tucked a cigarette behind his dark hair when Sutton refused.

"You know what I want right now?"

"What?"

"I want that cowboy hat I had that one day on the bay."

"I'm over there thinking about how we're gonna get back to the States and all you can think about is that fuckin' cowboy hat," Greg whistled as he exhaled a plume of smoke.

Sutton rubbed his shoulder, glanced over at his friend, and proceeded to flick the cigarette out of his hand. They laughed heartily and then uncontrollably as the adrenaline of their escape had only just now worn off.

"A cowboy hat, huh?" asked Greg.

"Yup, that's it."

"Plenty of those in Nebraska."

"I know. It's just pretty here. I like the pines."

"We have those, too."

"Not like here," responded Sutton.

"I hear you."

They prepared their food, gathered what wood they could, and set a fire where they sat. An occasional straggler here and there went by on the highway. One woman rode past on a horse with a child slung over the back. The woman's skin was burned, and the child was charred in a horrifying manner. When the wind shifted eastward, faint grey ash started to fall on the campsite. The ash was followed by ever-thickening smoke. Despite their fatigue, they put out their fire, finished what coffee they had in the pot, and mounted their tired horses to head overland away from the ash and away from the highway. More and more people on foot were making it into the area. It was time to leave anyway.

The pair rode for the better part of a day. It was slow going. Their horses were spent. They looked down from a ridge to see an old Bronco and two dirt bikes zipping noisily down the highway. These were the first vehicles they had seen since hitting the forest. Resting was not an option as the horizon behind them was clouded with smoke from a growing forest fire. Ash fell heavily and they did their best to cover their skin.

They were careful in their approach to their cabin, choosing the angle that would give them the best vantage if they had to make a run for it. The cabin was a smoldering heap. The vehicles of the bandits they'd encountered earlier in the week were nowhere to be seen. The pump house was burned down. Little remained aside from fencing and some foodstuffs strewn about.

Sutton shed a few tears. Their group had put so much hope into the place. Greg patted him on the shoulder and motioned to the Hobbit Hole. They lumbered onward, less alert than before. The sun was at its zenith and scorched them through the gray smoke that blotted out the sky. Greg stifled a cough when they walked into full view of a horse tied to the tree closest to their hidden cache. They drew their weapons.

"Who's there?" Sutton called out.

"Sutton?" the voice answered.

Sutton replied in the affirmative and Liam stepped out with a weary grin on his face. The friends rushed to their lost companion, embracing him and putting questions to him immediately.

"Where's Pietro?" asked Greg.

"No, he didn't make it. They put him in solitary for slapping one of the Officers. I didn't see him when I escaped. They had us at the airport for 'reeducation', but everything was in disarray. Pietro lost his temper. I kept quiet. Some of us broke into a vehicle bay in the night. We got to Government Island when they tracked us down. They didn't have drones so we jumped into the river."

Sutton whistled and said, "That's a steep drop."

"Me and one other guy, Martin, you know him – from Pod B, we made it. We weren't far from shore. His leg was broken. I helped him along through most of the night. We made it to his family's little place in Corbett. They gave me this horse and here I am. You saw the cabin, huh? I watched them do it.

Did you see the body? They shot one of their own in there before they burned it down. I've been here since late last night, hoping you guys'd show."

"Did you see the nukes go off?" Greg asked him.

"I counted two before I got into the mountains."

"We counted four."

"Jesus, honestly – I'd have thought there'd have been more."

"We need to head east. This is gonna kill us," Sutton wiped ash from shoulder.

"Your horses look assed out."

"So does yours. We've been pushing ours to the limit."

"Martin's people left me with some oats. That'll help a bit. Where to? Nebraska? You think Deseret will let us through?"

"We're not heading through Deseret. They'll string us up if they found out we were breeders. We know a guy in central Idaho. Has a cabin on a lake. Said he had plenty of food."

They hammered out the details of their trip to the best of their geographical knowledge, studied the map given to them, rested their horses for a couple of hours, and tested the few electronic devices in their cache to find them working but jammed. They reasoned it would take them a week to the cabin in Warm Lake, so long as there were no surprises. Eastern Oregon had been an impoverished wasteland ever since the poisoning of the major aquifer by the Matriarchy in response to a tax rebellion. After their rest, the men loaded their horses up and left on foot.

There was no raining ash in eastern Oregon. There wasn't much of anything, just dry foothills and sage brush. The trio rode their horses until the midday sun was unbearable and would post up under a dilapidated bridge or beneath a rocky outcropping. They learned the habit of turning over any rocks they planned to nap near.

"What do you want to do when you get home?" Liam asked Sutton.

Sutton pinched his lower lip as was his habit and pondered the question. "I have come to regret the way we lived. We were like high class prostitutes, weren't we?"

Greg nodded his assent to the proposition as he puffed on the last cigarette from the pack he'd scavenged.

"It was undignified."

"Come on, really?" Liam asked incredulously.

"Think about it. We were sexual commodities for them. They 'milked' us!"

"They paid us fabulously. I made in two years what would take me ten where I'm from."

"We all have more money, sitting in accounts somewhere," Greg said wryly.

"The money was good, we knew what we were signing up for, I know that," said Sutton. "I'm talking about the spiritual side."

Liam snorted.

"God fucking damnit, Liam, I'm getting at something here."

The tall blonde man steadied himself.

"I know we had it good. If we were born back there, we'd be eating bugs and getting operated on like everyone else. I just feel kind of empty, kind of used up. It's hitting me now. We all knew it was no good for us. I didn't think it'd feel this bad."

"We made it out," noted Greg.

"We did. I'm glad for that. It was just ugly and stupid, the whole thing."

"Would you trade the money to get your time back?"

"I'm a different person now so, yes. I would. I regret it. Seeing the city light up like that showed me how stupid and useless it all was. It was a city full of people eating bugs, trying to get famous, doing favors for people in government, and…"

"And worshipping death," added Greg.

"They were made that way, from birth. There's nothing we could have done to make things better for them," said Liam.

"Perhaps so, perhaps so. We profited off it, though," said Sutton.

"If we didn't, someone else would have. We were paid for existing. Better me than some other guy."

"All the other guys are dead now."

"You're right. Pietro was my best friend. That was one of the last functioning countries and look how shit things were. We got *something*. The rest of the fucking planet has gotten *nothing* lately. I'm glad we did it," said Liam.

"I see your point."

"There's no point in regret. There's no point in wishing you could take it all back. You're just coping because a lot of people just died, and your life was way better than theirs while you were living in proximity. That's it. Your moral conscience is operating on Nebraska rules when you stepped into a situation that was gone beyond all reason."

"I'm just tired" said Sutton.

"It happens to all of us, now and then," said Liam. "I felt regret the first time they strapped me to one of those machines during training month. I had the same thoughts you're having. Now, the question. What are you gonna do when you get back home?"

"Live better. Stay close to my family. Not jack off for like 10 years."

The men broke out laughing and toasted the prospect with their canteens.

Greg put the same question to Liam.

"I'm not going home," said Liam. "There's nothing there. All the guys on my team are gone. There's no money in it anymore. My mother's a bitch. My father's dead. My sister is in some haram in England. Seattle is dead, a hundred times over. They don't let you over the mountains if you were born west of them. Most of my money is here," he produced a small fob. "A year's pay is on here."

Sutton and Greg's jaws dropped.

"There's no way it works," said Greg.

"We'll see. I kept it wrapped. If it works, I'm rich as hell."

"They'll search you at the border if you come to Nebraska," said Sutton.

"Yeah, if we make it that far. If Mormons don't get us. I'll just stick it up my ass again. Still have the foil."

"I was grocery shopping when they announced the hard quarantine. No time to get home to mine," said Sutton.

"Same," said Greg.

"I'll make sure you guys are set up," Liam offered. "I'm telling you, I'm glad for the money. It's what has kept us from living like animals."

"It's the only thing."

"No, we're smart."

"Nobody else is going to do us any favors," said Greg.

"Nobody."

They closed down their conversation for the afternoon. Sutton had first shift on lookout. The other two went right to sleep. He looked out onto the barren landscape. The hills that rose up in the near distance were dark brown with volcanic rock peeking through in gradations from the scrubby grass that had lost all their color in the preceding years. There was a shack nearby with half of its metal roof missing. The entire thing was coated in dust and ringed by ancient weeds that looked as if they would crack into nothingness should a light breeze go through them.

The men decided to try for supplies in a small town called Huntington. They made the decision when on their approach to the Snake River, a tremendous wall of fortifications built from scrap metal and lumber rose up to greet them in the distance. Such a sight had been totally unique thus far. They approached the main gate with caution. A teenaged girl wearing a police uniform greeted them from atop the town gate.

"Hi there," she said. "State your business."

She produced a large caliber hunting rifle from behind the rampart.

"We're looking for supplies. I have a wound that needs disinfectant," said Sutton. "We'd love to rest our horses and we'd be happy to buy any feed you have." He motioned to Greg who produced a small bundle of bills from his shirt pocket and held them up for the girl to see.

"Walt," she called back to someone unseen person on the ground behind her. He didn't respond so she called again much louder for him. The trio of men thought they could hear music from a live band in the distance, somewhere in the bowels of the town. A balding middle-aged man with piercing eyes appeared from behind the ramparts, having walked up a set of steps to get a clear look at the visitors. He was dressed well despite the town's obvious poverty. He was much taller than the girl.

"You boys from Western Oregon?" he asked.

Sutton shrugged and replied in the affirmative.

Walk took the rifle from the girl and trained it on them, "You have ten seconds to leave."

"We're unmarked!" shouted Sutton. He ordered his friends to open their shirts and they did. "See, no tattoos, nothing. We were breeders. Us two are from Nebraska."

The man lowered his rifle upon recognizing the absence of tattoos, surgical alterations, and general femininity in the men mounted on horses before him. "Breeders, huh? Why didn't you say so? I was a breeder for two years, believe it or not. Jessie, open the gate for them." The girl did as she was told. A loud cranking sound could be heard. The progress was slow so Walt went down and helped the girl. He stepped out into view and apologized, "Sorry for the hostility. All this is new for us. Please, welcome to Huntington."

The men dismounted, helped Jessie close the gate, and shook hands with Walt. Walt whistled loudly through his teeth down into the town and a short, brown haired teenaged boy stepped out from the side of a house and ran up the road to the town gate. He told the boy to take his shift standing watch with Jessie and proceeded to lead the trio into town. "I'm the mayor here," he said. "Born and raised."

"I didn't think anyone was born and raised out here," observed Liam. "The John Day is poisoned and you're the first people we've seen in two days."

"The Snake's not poisoned." Walt glanced over to see the surprised look on the faces of his new companions. "You didn't know. I guess the Matriarchy would keep people in the dark about it. The John Day is only poisoned far downstream from the Columbia. You're right, there's hardly anybody out here. They used the basin for nuclear testing and internment camps. Didn't tell you that either, huh? The Columbia's clean so the Snake is clean. Think about it. Well, you weren't paid to think."

"I haven't had to think this much in years," said Sutton.

"Oh, I felt that way myself when my contract ended."

"Why is this town here?" asked Greg. He noticed a handful of elderly men along the way into town, each with a rifle at the ready and obscured from clear view.

"One of the original Matriarchs is from here. We were of sentimental value to her. She turned this town into a women's shelter, from what, I don't know. She's still got a house overlooking the river. Those old bitches have lots of secrets. Half of them have Chinese lovers. Golly, not a lot they told you! They'd let on some of this when I was a breeder. Of course, they were young enough to want sex back then. Their secrets shriveled up as they shriveled up, it would seem. Vale is another town they didn't bulldoze. There's one more south of the Steens but I've never been. Doesn't sound like Portland has fared well. We have word that everyone over there is…well…"

Sutton replied, "Nukes were going off when we were escaping the valley."

"Lots of infighting in the Matriarchy," noted Walt. "They kept you totally in the dark, it looks. Well, you were shrewd enough to make it this far. That whole city was a powder keg, by design. I think some of the original mothers saw what happened to Canada and decided to try their own version."

The four men rounded a corner and beheld a live band playing a song Sutton recognized from childhood, at the time it was already long out of fashion. The band was playing inside a small white gazebo with a red roof in what was the town's park. There was a small crowd of under a hundred people milling about the patch of grass ringed by trees. A stone's throw away there was a dilapidated train yard. The men crossed a pothole filled street and tied their horses to a rail attached to a brightly painted caboose that rested at the edge of the town park. Walt assured them no would steal from them when he saw Liam and Greg load spare ammunition into their pockets.

A voluptuous woman with fair skin exchanged a few words with Walt and her wary countenance changed dramatically. She led the newcomers to a table and plated them up with brisket, beans, and corn on the cob and served them cold beers. They devoured their food wolfishly. When he was sated, Sutton looked around and noticed the vast majority of the people gathered were old women. Liam was too busy chatting with the voluptuous woman, named Amy, to notice much else. Walt had gone into a shop across the street and was speaking with an old woman sitting in a chair by the shop door. Together they went inside and emerged with an assortment of supplies in a straw basket. The day went on with the town festival as the backdrop. People came and went, some talking with the visitors and others avoiding them like the plague. Sutton noticed a single Equality Officer looking woman being led around by two women armed with sidearms. There had been a mutiny in the town when it was clear Western Oregon would no longer be sending support or reinforcements of any kind. Walt had taken over as mayor, threatened exile to the lone representative of the Matriarchy in Huntington until two older women pleaded with him to keep her there on account of her fertile age, and pooled what labor there was in order to build the ramparts around the town. Help had come from the Idaho side of the river in exchange for half of the remaining fertile women, who were transferred out of town with little protest. No one in Huntington had heard from those men as their town was absorbed into a larger political body based out of Boise.

With the electrical grid down, able-bodied men were a commodity. This was apparent to the three men as Amy worked her charms on Liam. They talked late into the day until she excused herself to go to her home and tend to her garden. Liam approached Sutton, who was with their horses in a field, watching them graze.

"She sure wants you to stay," said Sutton. "She's about as good looking as they get." He snorted his approval as he had a strong buzz going from the beer he'd been furnished.

"The men are in charge here. You should stay, too. They've got housing, gravity irrigation and plumbing, and they think they can get the power back on eventually. Amy says it's a hell of a lot better than anything you're going to find between here and the Sawtooths."

"First time in a while I've seen a bunch of women let the men be in charge."

"They respect Walt. Amy told me his cognitive metrics. He's sharper than us. In his time, they made breeders do other work. She says he knows hydroelectric power systems really well and used to program drones before the EMP's. She's no slouch either."

"I feel like I can't even hardly fucking read after being in Portland so long," Sutton scoffed. "What a waste."

"There you go again."

"I know. It's not good. It'll wear off."

"That's why you should stay. Did you see that tall brunette? She was eyeing you."

"I can't even think about women. I'm so worn out on all that."

"Whatever floats your boat, bud. Pietro would take her in a heartbeat."

"You Seattle boys are different. No families, no prospects back home. Pietro would love it here. Greg and I are pressing on. We're going home after we stay with Paul's family at Warm Lake."

"Why not ride hard to Nebraska? They have spare horses here."

"I want some adventure, real adventure. Not the San Francisco bullshit they fed us in Portland. To me, it's romantic riding across the plains. When we were on contract you couldn't even take a dump without a robot coming out and testing it for substances. Everything digital. Everything digital, all the time. I'm glad the power went out. I feel like I'm getting my attention span back. They play *music* here, it's not just electronic trash with state messages in it…"

"What? You don't like *Snip It Off* or *We're All Queens*? I'm surprised, Sutton!" Liam said sarcastically. They were forced to listen to state sponsored pop music during their mandatory workouts. The women from their borough's women's professional soccer team were sometimes sent into the workouts to scream at and humiliate the breeders. The male-to-female soccer players were particularly vicious with the breeders. It was the worst part of the job.

Sutton cringed, his eyes going wide open, and he placed his palm over his crotch in a protective motion and inhaled sharply through his teeth to make Liam laugh.

"You know they're going to rely on you here," he said to his tall blonde friend after the moment had passed. "You can't just bang Amy and move on. They'll hang you for it. Walt's no joke."

"Oh, I know. Amy said I have to surrender all my possessions and work my way up from the bottom. Walt won't have it any other way and the other men are firmly with him."

"There's what, five of them altogether plus the old timers? We could take them," Sutton joked. "It blows me away the women aren't trying to run things here."

"The matriarch that kept the town going wanted it to be a women's shelter for the daughters and wives of ranchers. Those who wanted to stay in eastern Oregon could but only here and Vale. That's why the women are wholesome here. You shouldn't have had so much beer. You would have learned a thing or two."

"I say you come with us to Idaho."

"No, no, no. You should stay here. Idaho is rough country," Liam responded.

"Is that so? I thought all that was put down."

"It was, until this past week when everything went to hell."

"Any word on the United States, then?"

"Which set of them?" Liam referred to a collection of East Coast states that had formed their own 'United States' and the midwestern states from where Sutton originated.

"You know which ones I'm talking about."

"No word. The Deseret people control everything from east Idaho to the edge of Wyoming, since the grid went down. They have a quarantine going and nobody is allowed east into their territory. You guys are fine if you end-around."

"What the hell?"

"A Deseret missionary showed up in a diesel truck yesterday. He was recruiting anyone with medical credentials. He offered top dollar. That was all the information he gave. Territorial fuckers… He went back into Idaho. Walt says he teased him about going to Western Oregon."

"Oh yeah, how'd he respond to that?"

"He said everyone was dead out there."

"That's heavy."

"I bet it's the same where I'm from. I can't count on anything east of here."

"You can count on Nebraska. We had robots patrolling the border and more missile intercept systems on hand than stalks of corn. There's *no way* my country was nuked to oblivion. And, your money would actually mean something. You wouldn't have to just keep it in your butt," he teased his friend.

"Not worth the risk. Besides, your country hasn't flown any rescue and recovery planes our way yet. Deseret probably has them by the balls, somehow."

"You just want to screw Amy."

"Oh yeah. But I think it's more than that."

"Okay, what does Greg think?"

"He wants to screw her, too."

"Not what I meant. Bring me a beer, would you?"

"No, you've had enough, bud. Some of those people want to talk to you. You've been out here for two hours, watching the horses like a space case."

"I like having nothing to be distracted by."

"Greg's going with you."

"Good, I'm glad. I'll be social. Help me up."

As they left the field where the horses were fenced, Jessie from the town gate offered to brush their horses. She had a crush on Sutton and wanted to be of use to him. She was a pretty girl with dimples and freckles. Her beauty was not lost on the men and Liam was the most disposed toward her as he had less qualms with the lack of consent laws in Western Oregon than either Greg or Sutton had. But his sights were set on Amy. Sutton was reminded of his eldest brother's daughter upon looking at the girl. He smiled at her when she skipped girlishly to their horses, brush in hand. The horses took to her immediately.

The friends stayed two weeks in Huntington, helping with various projects around the town. They dug trenches. They helped erect a barn. They poured concrete. They fished for trout in the Snake. They went hunting for antelope in the foothills. For their work, Walt rewarded Sutton and Greg with Liam's horse as Liam had surrendered the horse so he could court Amy. He had already proposed to her and they were set to marry the night before Sutton and Greg would leave on their way into Idaho. The people of the town were happy to have another set of helping hands in Liam. The shock of so much societal uncertainty had the women worrying about the town's fertility. Many propositions were made to Sutton and Greg, including one woman undressing before them when the two were fishing in the river. She eyed them coyly, concentrating her gaze more so on Greg. Neither man wanted her as both were committed to finding their way to Nebraska. She blushed at the rejection, gathered herself, and walked away slowly, still hoping one of them would change their minds.

The few fertile women in the town petitioned Walt to drop his stringent standards for admission to the town, in order to entice Sutton and Greg. He refused steadfastly, citing the fact that the requirements were enshrined in the town charter. They complained that he had given Liam's horse back to the men to which he replied that as mayor he could delegate town resources as he saw fit, within budgetary constraints. They eyed Sutton and Greg greedily as they left in a huff, the men being nearby Walt most evenings.

The night of Liam and Amy's wedding arrived. It was held in an old Freemason hall that had been repurposed into a 'women's health clinic' when the Matriarchy deported all secret society members from their country. The clinic was gutted in the past months and slowly turned into a grange hall. The lone Equality Officer had protested and sent word back to Portland but no one there cared what happened in Huntington. The grange hall was blessed by an old man who had studied at Catholic seminary once upon a time and wandered into the town only the month prior as a kind of Christian holy man. There were no others like him as Christianity had long been outlawed in Western Oregon. His primary stipulation had been that he would not marry homosexuals to each other. This rankled several of the old lesbians in Huntington who had civil marriages through Western Oregon. Walt came to his defense and helped him override their objections. His threat to withhold his own unique skills much valued in the town also helped the cause.

"You sure?" Greg asked Liam as they sat around a side room in their best duds, waiting for the signal to walk up to the makeshift altar in the large hall.

"That's the second time you've asked, bud. Of course, I am. She's a sweet gal. Smart as a whip, too. It's a no brainer."

"Pietro's best friend becoming a family man, I never thought I'd see the day. You've bagged more women than those warlords in Europe. Does she know?"

"Know what?"

"That you've been around a bunch."

"She knows. Says she doesn't care. She says I'm funny, says that she never thought she'd meet someone with a higher IQ than herself. She was going to try for Walt in the fall if no one showed up from out west."

"Why didn't she leave?" asked Sutton.

"She was born here and her father before her. It's hard for her to leave. And the only ones this side of the Mississippi offering visas are Deseret. She hates the Mormons. They sold her father out to the Matriarchy. And they flooded their valley with foreigners."

"She has her point of view…" said Greg.

"Is that all it is?" Liam asked in an offended manner.

"Shit, you're right. Too much time in Portland. Too many of those bitches yelling at me. I apologize."

"No worries, bud. There's the cue. Let's go."

Sutton and Greg each happily patted Liam on the back and proceeded up to the altar. They wore borrowed shirts and slacks that didn't match. Earlier they had laughed at the sharp contrast in clothing quality from their recent life as breeders where they wore only tailored clothes from Singapore and other far-flung places now impossibly out of reach. An old woman sitting at a piano played a simplified arrangement by Liszt as Amy entered the hall wearing a white wedding dress that had been her mother's. She was radiant, her long reddish-brown hair flowing down her back. Her breasts swelled in the dress as it was just slightly too small for her frame. Her long legs and full backside looked fantastic as Liam sneaked a peak as she took her position across from him at the altar. Sutton caught the glance and marveled to himself that Liam didn't want a break from women as he and Greg did.

The officiant conducted the ceremony tastefully, though not a few people were left wondering if the old man ad-libbed a few parts. The bride and groom had rice thrown on them by the gathered townsfolk as they departed the grange hall for a potluck in the park. The town was unused to so many celebrations in such a short period of time and despite the average advanced age, much exuberance was shown. The relief at having some good news was enough to lift spirits. Though some had family in the

Willamette Valley, most did not and were relieved to be free of the oppressive yoke of the Matriarchy. Little sentiment was shown during the proceedings for the millions of lost souls on the other side of the Cascade Mountain Range. Seated at their prominent place in the banquet, Liam and Amy smiled as Sutton gave a brief toast as best man. He wished them many children, complimented the town, acknowledged Walt, and asked the bride to correct Liam if he ever slipped back into his 'Seattle ways'. Greg's toast was simple and to the point. He said Liam was one of the only sane people he had known since he left Nebraska and jokingly assured everyone in attendance that Liam, was in fact, not 'altered' in the colloquial sense of the word. The wedding party returned to the grange hall for an evening of music and singing. The few remaining fertile women continued to throw themselves at Sutton and Greg but they demurred. For their wedding night, Liam and Amy stayed in a historic cabin overlooking the Snake River. Sutton and Greg slept on their bed rolls out in one of Walt's pastures, to reaccustom themselves to sleeping on the ground. They planned to ride hard to Warm Lake since their horses were rested and they now had a spare.

The next day, Liam accompanied his departing friends to the bridge across the Snake River, beyond the ramparts of the town. He greeted them with two thumbs up and a hearty smile. At the start of the bridge they said their goodbyes.

"You still have your money?" Sutton asked Liam.

"Oh yeah," he said with a reassuring smile. "It's at Amy's place."

"Breaking their law already?"

"When everything's up and running again, I'll make sure it's put into the town. I have a lot of room to grow here," replied Liam. "Amy says to stay off 95. The tribes stalk it. They'd take your horses in a heartbeat."

"Walt told us."

"She also said to hook north to Sturgill Peak, if you can – best views in the area. There's a lookout there with supplies."

With that, the friends shook hands and Sutton and Greg started out over the bridge that had once carried trains but was repurposed to single vehicle passage. Sutton looked back to wave at Liam one more time. Amy approached at a distance on foot and waved to him. Sutton tapped Greg on the shoulder and they both waved for a moment to Amy. They had come to respect her in the brief time they'd known her. Sutton privately wondered when he would see Liam again. The significance of the departure dawned on him as it was the first time in his life he was unsure of seeing a loved one again. The reality of this disconnected, fragmented world hit home to him once again. In this spirit he cracked a joke to Greg about writing a letter to Liam.

True to their intent, they rode hard once they crossed into Idaho. They forewent the advice to go to Sturgill Peak, reasoning there'd be plenty to see when they got to Paul's. They made it to a river that night, seeing many more people on the way than they had in eastern Oregon. There was good grazing near the river. Their horses were ready to go in the morning and they rode hard again to the edge of the West Mountains. They made friends with a farmer named Harry Harrison who invited them to drink from a fresh spring on his property. They sat with him on his front porch and listened while he gently plucked a banjo. He could carry a conversation as he played. He asked question after question of Sutton and Greg on what had happened in Oregon. He was a prepper but had tired of the social isolation. He was in his early 60's. His skin was burned red from years in the sun. He wore a straw hat and his eyes were cast into a permanent squint that made him look confused. Beneath his straw hat he wore his brown hair short. The hat covered a balding spot he was no longer aware of as the years had gone by.

"Did you hear about the tax revolt a few years ago in this area?" he asked his visitors. They shook their heads. "It was big news," he tried again.

"We didn't get much news where we were," said Sutton.

"Tell me about it," responded Harry. "I went three months without speaking to another soul last year. This year it's different. Things are loosening up. Leadership in Boise got switched up. They ran the Mormons out in the last election. The tax revolt was part of what hurt them in the polls." He paused to set down his banjo. "They tried running up the property taxes in

Idaho's least populous counties. They switched a lot of properties off of agricultural zoning. My tax tripled. A bunch of us rode into Council and took over the County Courthouse. They had some Mormon idiot presiding as sheriff. He was a Pacific Islander, originally. We held him hostage. We were in there a week negotiating with Boise when a bunch of other counties started doing the same. Up in Boundary County they executed all the tax officials. Once folks from other counties started stepping in and doing their part, Boise backed off. Some homosexual Mormon in their tax agency got sacked. He was sending the funds down to Deseret. It was pure madness. Who ever heard of such a thing? But the state legislature was bought off and the natives were going nuts cause they finally got tired of missing out on the Federal payments that were coming in when we were still in the United States. Nobody goes to their stupid casinos anymore. They wised up, got arms brought in from Western Oregon of all places, and started raiding the highways like it was the 1800's. You still can't get further than Riggins up on 95. To get to Coeur D'Alene you have to fly and hope those idiots in Missoula don't shoot you down. Or you try for eastern Washington and hope the Mexican cops don't fuck you in the ass. Everything's all gone to hell and it's the only preoccupation people have anymore. But you boys have been living the high life over there in Portland. I'm sure you're not worried."

"We're learning to be," said Greg. He leaned down and pet Harry's Australian cattle dog.

"Nebraska's a long ways away, real far away…" Harry mused. "Especially with no flights. I believe you. I haven't had power in almost a month. Always figured the powers that be would fuck with it, anyway. No planes, no cars. I've been here 25 years, waiting for this. Now that it's here, I don't know what to do. I'm estranged from my children. Should never have sent them to the government schools. Last I heard, my daughter was going to marry a black. My son declared he was gay when I first came here. I disowned him. The stupidest mistake of my life was letting the courts separate me from them. Their mother corrupted them. I'm squarely in a midlife crisis. Hell of a time for it to hit."

"You did the preparedness part right," offered Sutton.

"But it ain't no good without family. Sorry to depress you boys. Don't get a lot of visitors here."

"No, we're happy for the company after the shitshow we've been through."

"What'd you make of Portland?" Harry asked Greg.

"They fed us well. We didn't want for anything up until a few months ago when the wheels started to come off on their funding. One of our overseers was on their women's soccer team."

"Which one?"

"The meanest one. The one with the short, pink hair that was always speaking at rallies in Pioneer Place."

"The captain of the team! I saw her on the cover of a magazine a couple years ago. Those bitches have a lot of power over there. They did a profile on them that made it seem like they were small time dictators or something."

"They were," said Greg. "They weren't allowed to knock us around much. You know, precious cargo," he grabbed his crotch, "but they sure could yell at us. That was the worst part of it. Some of it was fun. They kept some of their nature conservation areas clean and neat. We did some hiking."

"We did a lot of boating," said Sutton.

"A lot of that. We were pampered, for sure. And they kept us in tip-top shape. Like boot camp but a portion of your time is hooked up their 'milking' machines. When we were first on contract the machines had screens that would play porn. Whatever you liked; it was customized. In the past year they started putting advertisements in. You couldn't shut off the screens. It was exhausting."

"They were milking you for sperm? What the fuck? You were breeders?" asked Harry. "I thought that was an urban myth."

"Oh no, it was very much real."

"You're not queers are you? Porn makes you gay."

"Oh no, definitely not swinging that way," Greg replied.

"Everyone's something strange over there. Well, everyone *was*. Now they're all dust particles in the atmosphere!" He laughed hoarsely and kicked off his boots. "I'm downright surprised they didn't do any surgeries on you two."

"None of that. The Matriarchs wanted the men 'unaltered'. The guy who runs Huntington west of here, Walt, he was in the first generation of breeders. They did surgeries and hormones on a few of them but quit as soon as they saw the results."

"Pure madness to hold two opposing ideas like that: hormones and surgery for all the boys born in your country but you keep a harem of pretty boys untouched so they can provide sperm stock for your higher ups. Fuckin' government."

"We're learning as we go," said Sutton.

"What? They didn't teach you proper values in Nebraska? That's one of the most fascist places I've ever been to."

"We were both homeschooled. We didn't have to worry about all this Portland shit. Our families had businesses and that's what we learned."

"Well, no wonder you took the contracts. Contracts…contracts to have machines suck your dicks a few times a week. That's the damndest thing. I knew they were doing that shit over in Asia. Didn't think they'd bring it to America.

Well, look what those dykes in Western Oregon sowed for themselves. They nuked their own country because they didn't want to have to give it up to the Chinese. Reaped what they sowed. I always hoped those soccer dykes would die in a plane crash or some shit."

Sutton and Greg were shocked at the man's blunt opinionating. Harry looked over from his rocking chair to the dumbfounded looks on their faces.

"Oh, so you're smart enough and tough enough to smuggle yourself out of a nuclear holocaust but you can't see how twisted and fucked up those people were. For having high IQ's, you two sure are peckerheads. I've never met anyone so naïve. Wait, I take that back. I knew some Mexicans who wanted to start a Catholic mission in Deseret so they could bring their family members up. Now *those* people were peckerheads. You better learn quick if you're gonna make it in the new world order that's arriving. We're entering a feudal era. All those Satanic elites are gonna start calling the shots from their underground cities. They'll be trading children like baseball cards, everything out in the open. They started in Denver. Child escort markets. Then there were the Panics. Here, Deseret, and your country are the only good places left. My idiot kids will probably sell their kids. The pedophiles pay less for mixies because the parents are too stupid and brainwashed to put up a fight anyway. I should have never married their mother. Thank God, I have a brother with his head on straight. His kids will carry on the family name."

"Why isn't your brother here?" asked Greg.

"He's got business in South Dakota. He runs a mining outfit in the Black Hills. He was one of the first prospectors to move in after all the folks on the reservations got sick and died out. I couldn't ever respect him with the way he made his money. It drove a wedge between us."

"But you told us the natives around here are marauders," noted Sutton.

"Yeah, but the ones up there and in Sheridan were good folks. It's a crying tragedy what happened to them. I'd take ten of them before I took a Mexican. Casinos or drug crime and rape epidemics? I know which one I'm picking."

"Why do you think America fell apart?" Sutton asked Harry. Harry was taking on a teaching role to these young men. Sutton had heard a smattering of the man's opinions before from his own brothers but as they moved away from the family business, he had become more and more engrossed in the work before the breeder contract appeared suddenly on his horizon. He wasn't in the slightest ideological, nor were his parents, and after two years in the hyper-politicized Western Oregon environment, he was curious to see an alternate viewpoint. He pinched his lower lip as he focused on Harry's response.

"They didn't teach you in school? Oh wait, you were homeschooled. When I was a boy, we made fun of homeschooled kids. Maybe you got the better end of the stick, though. America fell apart because there too many people from too many different cultures and races in the same place. The blacks took over whole cities, there'd be a huge crimewave, everyone would blame it on the politics of the blacks instead of their violent natures, and the cycle would repeat itself. Same with the Mexicans in the south. That's why the California border is up south of San Francisco. All the Mexicans brought drugs, child abuse, and other low IQ shit with them. That's why New Mexico and half of Arizona are part of Mexico now. That's why Nevada damned near broke away with them until the governments struck a deal to deport all the Mexicans there. It's why Texas had another civil war. It's why there were race wars in the South. It's why your part of the country has exclusionary laws. And don't get me started on all the Chinese that took over the west coast or the never-ending bloodbath that Europe has become. When I was a boy, we had family in Germany we visited once. There were still mostly just Germans there and things were peaceful. The same with America. It used to be mostly just "Americans". It was a bi-racial thing: us and the blacks, and most of whom had a little bit of white blood in them. Before I was born, they changed the laws on that and started letting in anyone who had problems, anyone from a failed nation. They stopped checking for health problems just before the collapse, that was when you two were probably just born. The country buckled and split. Three Presidents in a row were assassinated, from both sides. Alternative currencies were banned. The techno-pedophiles took over whole major cities. Nukes. You boys know the rest, don't you?"

"My father told me some," said Greg.

"Most everything had fallen into place right when you were born. You're lucky. Up until the past couple years, things were peaceful for a while. Everyone went their separate ways. But, when power consolidates, the government gets greedy and conquests start happening. Look at Africa: the whole continent is a slave society for the Chinese. They took over the whole thing, most of it through debt ownership. Why do you think they snapped up half of Washington and everything west of the Rockies in Canada? The only people strong enough to hold back these demons are here, Deseret, or the Reformed United States. I can't believe those lesbos in Western Oregon had a country for as long as they did. I think they got big funding from California. I think it was the Californians who nuked the place when they couldn't hold onto it."

"Where do you learn all this?" asked Sutton. His head was spinning from the information, yet he felt his world snapping into place. Events and circumstances he'd noticed only on the periphery were expanding into the forefront of his awareness.

"Your free press. They allow the information to proliferate here. We don't have much going because Boise's the biggest city and we cleared out all our troublemakers, we'll call them, during the collapse. Deseret has a lid on their situation. Our Rocky Mountain Federation is your closest ally. When we lost our access to the Pacific, your country stepped in with some damn good trade deals that kept us alive. Of course, it didn't matter much to me because I've got enough food and ammo here to last me the rest of my life. But it was good to see white men come together and honor their common heritage for once. We're like 2% of the world's population after the rivers of blood that washed Europe out."

"So you're racist?"

"Racist! That's a made-up word. Jesus, your parents didn't teach you that? Or were you brainwashed to hell when they had those dick-sucking machines on you? Racist, my ass. You must've picked that up from Portland."

"We had a few classes during intake," said Greg. "White people are at fault for the United States breaking up, is what they said. We paid reparations out of our paychecks. The non-white neighborhoods were the nicest in Portland."

"Those matriarchs were skimming off the top of that, I can promise you that. What a racket. Always the race racket."

"What do you mean?" asked Sutton.

"Your country has immigration quotas on race. Why do you think they're there? It's to keep the crime low and the trust high. You ever wondered why the Reformed United States takes in 90% of its people from Europe?"

"I never thought about that."

"You wouldn't, living where you were, I guess. The only countries worth living in anymore have missile defense systems, extreme border security, and immigration quotas that take into account intelligence and race. It's why Poland, Hungary, and Italy are the only countries left standing in Europe. It's why your country has been shrewd enough to keep its corridor open to the Gulf of Mexico. It's why China and Israel are the world powers and it's why Japan fell. You can't have more than two races living in one country. One needs to have the majority and the two can live in courteous harmony. That's why there's so-called peace in the Great Lakes: the black Muslims run everything and keep the whites around so their infrastructure doesn't completely fall apart. It was the same deal with your matriarchs and the Chinese until the lesbos lost their majority. Same with us here and the Mexicans. Deseret is going to be the next shithole to explode. You can't have African communists blowing up your factories and getting into street wars with Mexicans and Pacific Islanders. Deseret won't last another two years, especially if the pedophiles who run Denver can get their EMP's through."

"We hate Denver," said Greg. "*That* is something we do know from back home."

"When I was a boy, it was the Mexicans who were running drugs into Denver – not the other way around."

"What are you going to do out here, wait until the world ends? Or what about making peace with your brother?" asked

Sutton as he stood up and grabbed a stick to play tug o' war with Harry's dog.

"I'm sure we'll get around to it. He's got two sons and a daughter about your age. They're the next best thing, compared to my kids. I came out here from Colorado because I knew the air and water would be clean. No Communists poisoning the water out here. No Satanists bumping and grinding with children at musical festivals. Nobody ever gave a shit enough about this neck of the woods to come and fuck with it. There are rumors of a couple of pedophile outfits as far out as Sun Valley, but I think it's just rumors. I'm gonna take my time out here, finish writing my book, see what shakes out with the power situation, and if my brother and I decide to patch it up, I'll buy passage through Wyoming with the crypto I have left and see if he'll have me back. You can buy land with gold in South Dakota. I've got plenty of it from before the wars, buried. That's confidential," he added morosely. The truth was that he was more than ready to leave his corner of the world and find his way back to his brother. The newfound information that the territory west of him had vanished in a nuclear cloud gave him great concern that his home would soon see the dreaded fallout that had already ravished large swaths of the continent. A part of him wanted to ride out with these young men.

"You're not happy out here?" asked Sutton.

"Happy? Sure, plenty happy. I don't like most people but I like people. Don't know if that makes sense but that's how I see it. Most people are evil. We saw that when America, the old one, was falling apart. Everyone was in it to make a buck. The most immoral ones were the ones who rose in that society. When your country is dying from legalese and whoever controls the narrative through the media, only the ones who can shut out their moral conscience and their Christian sense of decency can make it. It takes sociopaths to fight sociopaths. All the quiet went out of the world. People did that. Whether it was the intellectual titans running their best manipulations at the end, the technophile child molesters, or the ravenous hordes – humankind ran all semblance of goodness out of the world. If you listen closely, you'll catch it in pockets here and there. It used to be everywhere there was countryside, but they all got hip to that and ran fiber lines all over, even where it wasn't in their financial interests. Bring in the noise, put the fear into everyone, divide people whether through race baiting or open tokenism, and when the dollar fails – pow! -you've got open revolutions and a cavalcade of reasons to practice whatever sin you've harbored in the darkness of your heart. All of this mess has just been an excuse to hurt the children."

"You're writing a book about all this?" asked Sutton.

"More or less. I don't know who I'm writing it for. I thought it could be for kids, but no parent teaches their kids these lessons. I'm probably too bitter over my own failures as a parent. I failed to protect them from their mother, not like she didn't have a heavy helping hand in all of it. If the power grid was down *then*, it wouldn't have played out the way it did.

They'd be safe and sound with me if they were young now or however you figure it. But that doesn't excuse my weakness. Maybe it's a book for young men such as yourselves, men with some fight left in them. You may be naïve as hell and have yet to learn the way of the world, as late into adulthood as you are for such a thing, but you managed to survive Portland without turning into total queers. It's encouraging to see you make for Nebraska, come hell or high water. Don't have a clue how I'm going to distribute the thing. Had to switch to a typewriter and when the ink runs out on that, it'll be pen and pad like it was in my great-grandfather's day."

Sutton regarded this funny old man wearing a baseball cap bearing the name of a long defunct tractor company. He seemed as far removed from cosmopolitan life as possible. His face had deep crow's feet from his refusal to wear sunglasses. The skin on his neck was permanently red from his long hours outside, rain or snow. Sutton liked him and trusted him as he mirrored back to him shades of the men he had grown up around in rural Nebraska, though those men were far less racially or societally aware. This man knew much more of the world than the farmer types in Nebraska, who had become jet-setting entrepreneurs in the Reformed America era of agricultural self-sufficiency and year after year trade surpluses. Yet he retained a shut-in, hermit-like energy about him. Sutton wondered if the man had spent too much time on the Internet in his formative years, back when the Internet wasn't a complete sewer of corporate information and all-pervading government censorship. That was the most sense he could make out of the man.

"Let me ask you fellas something," said Harry. "Did either of you, at any point in your lives, wonder if there was something seriously wrong with the world? Something deep and practically immovable that shifted everyone's decisions in an ugly direction, something akin to living in a simulation where the truth could never be attained."

Sutton was the first to reply, "I never had a sense of righteousness about America falling apart. I guess I never experienced what was so good about it and never had anything to compare to."

"Who can fault you? Nebraska is about as cozy as it gets, especially after your lot put IQ tests to everyone in Omaha and booted out the dummies. And you, Greg?"

"I haven't thought about it in a long time because I was young, maybe seven years old. I remember something that happened to my father and me. He took me on a trip to Philadelphia for his birthday. The son of one of his local buddies from back in the day was with us, too. Trevor. We didn't know that one of the first Great Panics was going to happen that day. He wanted to take me to a restaurant where he used to go every day for lunch in high school. The city had just passed an ordinance where white men further apart in age than five years couldn't be sitting together in public, private establishments, and so forth. We had to go everywhere by car and gas was expensive. To eat at the restaurant, we had to sit separately and talk over the phone. Some Asian girl was watching her tablet loudly. One of my favorite commentators had just sold out and was cross-dressing on camera with a blonde wig on. This was a guy who was pretty principled and one of the last who'd managed to speak out about anything that mattered, before the censorship was everywhere. Trevor and I couldn't believe what we saw. I laughed out loud. The girl caught me looking at the tablet. She screamed out for help. There were two cops eating there nearby. They were openly homosexual, so the ban didn't apply to them. They had a minder from the controlling party there in Pennsylvania, he was white but not white. I don't know if that makes sense. They came over and started questioning us. We didn't answer them, like my father taught us. One of them pulled his penis out of his pants and started rubbing it across my back. This I knew was deeply wrong. It was in this moment that the Great Panic started. All the screens everywhere, including the girl's tablet, switched over to that garbled electronic music. Did you ever hear it? Yeah, it sounded straight out of hell. The major pop queen the Satanists were pushing was screaming and started stabbing a small child to death. She was screaming that nuclear war was breaking out, that America was dead, and that the Satanists had taken over food distribution and nobody would get anything to eat anymore. Everyone in the restaurant freaked out because only important messages from the government overrode all broadcasts back then, at least how my father recounted it to me later when we got to safety. He saw the cop was abusing me and how the other cop was starting to work on Trevor. Everyone was panicking except the cops and their minder. My dad rushed over, clubbed the cops with a chair, and pulled us out of there. The cops came running after us. He tripped the first one, who was tall as a tree, and stomped his face when the other one jumped on his back. Trevor and I cried and crouched against the building. The whole city went nuts. We had no idea that broadcast went out across the entire country. Before that, the Satanists were treated like some fringe group that only held a few seats in Congress. Now everyone realized how much power they had and why the President had that pop queen accompany him everywhere. We always saw her doing innocuous things in the news but she was ringed by those bearded drag queens, remember them? Seeing her murder a kid with a huge butcher knife and say everything she did just put it into everyone's mind that America really was going to fall apart. There was looting instantly. People fought over everything. And the Satanists weren't kidding, we saw semi-trucks turn in place, crush everything in their path, and head out of the cities south to Virginia and wherever else they had their 'production facilities', the ones with the huge bunkers underneath. My dad knocked the second cop off his back, knocked him out with a punch, and we ran back to our car. The car was smashed up already. We were standing there, thinking of what to do next when Trevor's dad showed up in a school bus. Yeah, I'm not kidding. It was all reinforced and kept in a parking garage in the city at massive expense to the guy. He had a few families on board with him, people from his apartment building. We jumped in. We plowed through everything that was in our way. Soldiers at a checkpoint started firing into the bus, we drove right through them. I still remember them screaming as their bodies went under the big tires. Satanists came out into the open and were stabbing everyone. It was a gun-free city, so it was a slaughter. I didn't realize there were thousands and thousands of them. The roads were pretty empty at that point because gas was so heavily rationed. We drew some negative attention coming into Philadelphia but it was a whole nother experience going out of the city."

"Moral of the story: stay the fuck out of the cities," said Harry.

"When we took our contracts in Portland, they promised us there would be no Panics. I guess, in a sense, they were right."

"Terrible thing to happen to you so young," said Harry. "In Colorado they dosed all the kids in the schools with psychedelic mushrooms and put them into gymnasiums to watch the Great Panic. The media painted it like it was funny. The late night hosts would use it as 'viral footage'."

"Yeah, they did that wherever we went. Everyone was saying it was funny."

"Thank God the country was already broken apart at that point," said Sutton.

"We drove like hell to Columbus, crossed the border, and never went back to the east. They took Trevor and his dad as asylum seekers. They settled in Wichita."

"You know, the Christian Knights assassinated that pop queen," said Harry. "The woman you see in the advertisements is just special effects, or a clone. I don't know which. If the head of Amazon can clone himself, you bet your ass that other Satanists have done the same for themselves. The world's too kooky outside our brother nations."

"In Western Oregon they showed her as a Matriarch sister. I never made the connection," said Greg.

"Makes sense."

"Did you fight in any of the wars?" Sutton asked Harry.

"I was militia for a bit but no action, not me. I knew I didn't want to fight. The tax revolt was as crazy as it got for me. That's not altogether rare when you consider how many folks settled out here before the country split up. A lot of guys like me wanted the society of our grandfathers and we figured if we just chose better laws, ones that excluded the kinds of people we didn't want in a society, then we'd be fine. The results speak for themselves. We have a nation here where we see outside nations as hostiles and competitors, even you folks in the Reformed. We uphold our sovereignty upon pain of death. But it's also a shitshow where nothing works. Too many stupid people. Kind of like the Confederate States, once upon a time."

"We killed people getting out of Portland," said Greg.

"You did what you had to do, I'm sure," said Harry.

"Did you ever kill anyone?"

"I think I did. In Colorado I shot a Mexican in the gut. He keeled over in a bad way, gasping and all that. I didn't stick around to see if he lived but the chances are low with two .45 ACP rounds in your lower intestines."

"What did he do?" asked Sutton.

"He looked at me in a way I didn't like."

"That's it?"

"No, I was being facetious. He bought a house in the neighborhood I was living in. He was trafficking people into Colorado. You could see them in his backyard sometimes. He was moving drugs, too. I know what he and his men were doing to those women they were bringing into the country. I kept it real friendly with him. When it was time for me to move out of there, I shot him as he was bringing his garbage can in from the street, popped back into my car, and hit the road."

"Did you do it because of his race?" asked Sutton.

"God, I don't think so. I did it because I was bitter over losing my kids and cause it seemed like the right thing to do at the time. That was when everyone was taking the law into their own hands. I did what a million other people have done since then. Now, his race is more inclined to violence than ours but no, I wouldn't do that to someone. Governments do that kind of thing, especially to white people. We grin and bear it like idiots."

Greg and Sutton both agreed it was time for sleep. Harry was happy to show them to their cots in a dry bunkhouse near his stables. The older man took his customary walk with his dog around the perimeter of the property, armed with a shotgun and a sidearm. He invited the young men to stay however long they wanted as he trudged away. The sky was full of bright stars and the air was cool and reassuring.

In the morning the travelers decided to stay one more night with Harry. Dinner had been decent enough and they were curious to hear more of his stories. Sutton commented that he felt as if he were getting an education in the things his parents were reluctant or neglectful to say. Inwardly, Greg was relieved to be spending time with a man who was against homosexuality. The lifestyle had been pressed onto him anytime he left the "pod" for breeders in Portland. Advertisements for coffee shops would feature enlarged penises piercing through donuts. Several of the professional women's soccer teams had homosexual men as their mascots. In Western Oregon, homosexuality had been promoted but also treated as a lesser sexual orientation than lesbianism. Remembering the lucrative pay of his contract as a breeder, Greg had continually swallowed down the disgust he felt at the cacophony of lewd sexual acts performed in public that he'd been exposed to on errands as simple as buying snacks that weren't available in the breeding center cafeteria. Homosexuality was not only not allowed back home in the Reformed United States, but it also wasn't legally enshrined as a preferable orientation, as was the case in most of the rest of the continent aside from Deseret and the Federation, within whose borders he now found himself. Harry's frank and open intolerance for homosexuality, his coarse questioning in suspicion of potential homosexuality when the two travelers had first greeted him and asked to pass through his property, and his casual use of vulgar, derogatory terms for the orientation put Greg at ease with his feelings of disgust. This was a man he would not have to hide his true feelings from. The experience, for him, was relatively novel. In the past he had only felt at ease with those who were similar to him in age and vocation. Sutton's familiarity to him rarely ranged outside of the habitual and into the ideological. Sutton wasn't ideological. Nor was Liam, nor had Pietro been. Pietro came the closest to idealism but was driven out of boredom. Greg had touches of it, here and there. His father had told him only a thing or two.

Harry put the pair to work digging holes for fence posts and when that was done, they helped him cart a load of firewood to an elderly neighbor couple that was past the age of doing such work for themselves. In exchange, the old woman fixed them up a jar of mint lemonade and two smaller jars of sauerkraut she swore would set them right. They graciously accepted her gifts before riding back to Harry's place on the trailer he'd turned into a makeshift horse-drawn cart. Semi-automatic rifle fire could be heard in the distance, but Harry waved off the concern he saw in the young men.

He turned his eyes back to the road and said, "That's the Bridger Outfit. They have a compound up there. Don't worry, we got things a lot more sorted out here in Idaho than where you've been. They're running their kids through shooting drills. Why they're doing it in the heat of the day beats me but they have their own notions of how to do what they're doing. I'm old and want a nap when it gets to this point in the day. Should've asked Lucy to send us off with glasses, too. Lemonade and a nap: that's the ticket. We can visit the Bridger folks, if you want. The kids love anything Lucy fixes up."

They turned toward the source of the gunfire and headed up a winding road flanked by sagebrush and dead grass. The Bridger compound appeared suddenly as the cart rounded a bend. A man was already walking out to greet Harry and his companions. The man commented to Harry that it had been far too long and he ought to try and be less of a hermit. The compound was a small collection of mobile homes and one large red barn situated in the center. A tall stone wall was clearly in the process of being built and formed a u-shape around the backside of the property. The property backed up against a hill that backed up to much taller hills. The man shook Harry's hand, introduced himself to the travelers, and after the horse was unhitched and led to a pasture with other horses, the men all made their way to where the children were being taught to shoot by their elders. The Bridger Outfit, as it was formally dubbed, was established a decade prior by two brothers who were linemen in Orofino and then Cambridge nearby. They pooled their resources with two friends of theirs and established the compound in the interests of sustainable, communal living. The compound had once served as an outfitting camp, hence its name. The founding brothers were named Joe and Henry. Their friends were Thad and Dan. Each had a wife and at least two kids. A woman from Western Oregon also lived there with an infant. It was unclear who among the men she was adjoined to but she'd been there over a year, so it was one of them. Thad and Henry were busy with the children. Joe did most of the talking to the visitors, putting the same kind of questions to Sutton and Greg that Harry had. Such mutual defense and aid compacts were common, especially in frontier regions between the various nations that once comprised George Washington's United States. With the power down, the irrigation canals in the area had seen their flows go down. Much work was being done to make the changeover to gravity fed irrigation and to dissuade anyone in the area from the temptation of flood-irrigating their crops as it would choke off anyone down the line. This summer would be a difficult one and if the power couldn't be brought back, the compound had enough supplies to last three years. In the meantime, they would make alternative arrangements for irrigation. This contingency was not altogether unanticipated.

Harry's reason for staying, as opposed to going off on an adventure with Sutton and Greg, was his growing sense of duty to his neighbors. His own situation involved years of rainwater collection, a seasonal spring on his property, and a single person to collect water for. It wasn't so much that he liked his neighbors, as he hardly spent time with them, he simply felt a duty to see them through what their most difficult trial had been up to this point. He liked being useful to others, in spurts, when his books and his contemplation allowed for it.

When the mint lemonade was doled out and not a drop remained, the men left the children to play, and put hours of work into trench digging for the piping that would carry a small rivulet out of the irrigation canal and into the waiting gardens down a brief slope. Henry's wife brought smoked trout on a plate from the food stores and commented to Sutton and Greg that if they at any point they happened upon a working inverter or controller for a solar system and sent it back, the Bridger Outfit would be in their deepest debt. The small military of Deseret had a maniacal zeal for bombarding neighboring nations with EMP bombs before running caravans of missionaries through with the requisite replacement electronics essential for rural living. The price for salvation was conversion and tribute. A missionary had been seen in the area in a diesel truck, oftentimes a precursor for a strike. The Outfit would not be converted as all the adults were devout Catholics. Nor would many of the families in the area be willing to give up their faith, so perhaps Sutton and Greg would pay lip service to the tribute and come out with some functioning electronics they could funnel back to the compound. The consideration was noted, the wife thanked the visitors, and their work on the trench digging resumed.

Work was eventually was paused for a late lunch of sandwiches made entirely of fresh ingredients from the Bridger place. This was the first such meal of which Sutton and Greg had partaken. There was political talk, but it soon slipped that the woman from Western Oregon had had her child with Thad. His wife had approved soon after the woman had been taken in and no suitors were found in the area. The woman, Morgan, had been a nurse previously and thus held a skillset not possessed by anyone at the compound. Sutton and Greg quietly cursed Thad's luck when they both went on a pee break.

"You see how good looking that guy's women are? He has two of them," said Sutton to his nearby friend.

"The rich get richer. This place is what we wanted our cabin to be like. Thad's living it right. Who the fuck bodybuilds in a post-apocalyptic society?"

"Harry doesn't look too thrilled about Thad's situation," Sutton commented on the man's obvious dour demeanor and clipped dissenting comments when conversation had turned to Morgan.

"Harry's careful."

"He's too careful. I would love to have two women," said Greg.

"You had that all the time and more in Portland. The matriarchs were freaks."

"On the regular, is what I'm saying," Greg replied as they headed back to the group.

"Having sex with two women is one thing, dealing with their emotions is another. No way, not for me," said Sutton to close out the conversation.

When the work was finished for the day, Harry and his visitors were enjoined to come back anytime. Harry was non-committal. His aloof habits were well-ingrained. Sutton made mention of Warm Lake for the first time and promised to return with any electronic components the Outfit could use. Henry's wife gifted Sutton and Greg an air sealed bag of smoked trout on their way out. The children tagged alongside the wagon for a minute before being called back by one of the women. Further goodbyes were waved, and the wagon rolled out of sight.

"Sweet people," said Harry.

"They sound like they could use you around more often," Sutton floated the suggestion to the older man. "There's no grandparents there."

"I guess so," said Harry as he placed a hand on his cattle dog seated beside him. "That'd be something for an old fart like me."

The night came and went with little fanfare as Harry retreated to his cabin out of exhaustion. He lay awake, thinking of the great adventure before his visitors and how he wished he could go with them. He would not, though, as the realities of his physical agedness were upon him. He kept tubes of painkiller gels in one of his root cellars. They were prescription medications he'd bought off a doctor who was leaving Idaho early on in Harry's life on the brushy plains. His back was sore from being too tall. His knees ached from the years of labor around the place. His visitors wouldn't consider living at his property or at a place like the Bridger Outfit. There weren't any single women. They'd have to make their way to Boise, Deseret, or back to their home country before finding single women in any kind of abundance. Or they'd have to strike it lucky with some pair of sisters from some mountain commune that would let down their guard enough to let them in – and that was if they weren't fervently religious. No, they would be on their way in the morning. Harry knew he lived in isolation but he wasn't ready to give it up yet. If anything, the signs all pointed toward more cataclysms to come. Would there be fallout this far east from the Willamette Valley? Would Deseret decide to spread out into this relatively unprotected corner of the Federation? Would there be any more grey winters? He took solace in the knowledge that the pedophiles wouldn't target him on account of his age, the

Mexicans wouldn't settle nearby because even with irrigation the land wasn't arable enough to entice them, and the tax system would go down in flames with no running electricity within a hundred miles. He could live and die in this place he had chosen for himself decades before. An uncle of his had lived most of his life in Idaho. A second cousin was probably still alive somewhere near Spokane. This was as familiar a place to Harry as any could be and aside from the prospect of reconciling with his brother, this would likely be it for him. The suggestion that he join the Bridger Outfit provoked him more than he thought it would for he knew he would need someone to care for him in his old age. He didn't like the idea of sharing his vast stores of food, ammunition, and medicine with anyone but since he had taken the risk of sharing knowledge of their existence with his visitors, he figured he would have to share eventually whether he liked it or not. The vitality of these young, strong men humbled him in his considerations of riding across Idaho, around Wyoming, and somehow making it up to South Dakota. He took a pain pill he'd been keeping on his nightstand and swallowed it down with some water. His dog whined knowingly.

In the morning, Sutton and Greg were loading up their horses between bites. Harry sat in his rocking chair, petting his dog and hiding his sadness. He thought about playing his banjo to distract himself. When he sensed they were close to being finished, he went inside and produced gifts for the two. He walked up to Sutton and handed him a straw cowboy hat. Sutton gasped involuntarily as the hat was handed to him.

"This may not fit but I have spacers," he said.

The hat fit Sutton like a charm.

"You sure?" Sutton asked boyishly.

"I got a few more. You want one?" he asked Greg.

"Please!" was Greg's response.

Harry went back into his cabin and produced another hat, straw as the other one but with sharper lines and a wider brim. The fit was loose on Greg's head so Harry put two strips of foam adhesive strips onto the band and the fit became snug.

"Here, there's this as well," said Harry as he took a row of five packs of unfiltered cigarettes that were adhered together by a plastic film and handed it to Greg. "You said you picked up the habit. I don't need them."

"I better not," Greg said self-consciously. "Bad for me."

"You can trade them. They're worth a lot to some people. I've had them in an airtight container for twenty-five years. These are pre-war. No nothing on them."

"I can't thank you enough," said Greg.

"Write me whenever the mail comes back," said Harry. "Tell me what you did with them."

"I can't thank you enough either," said Sutton, making a show of tipping his new hat to Harry. He hid his elation, but it wasn't enough to stop a smile from coming across his self-serious host's face.

"Wearing those things would get you killed anywhere but where you're going. Our kind may be dying out but there's enough good people along the way that'll see you for who you are. Once upon a time a crucifix would ward away vampires, at least in the stories. Those should bring you two good luck."

The host and his parting company shook hands. Sutton rang the bell on the log arch at the entrance of Harry's property and waved one more time before riding away with his friend on the county road that would lead them north and east to their next stop. Harry sighed and wiped a tear from his eye. He walked back to his study in his cabin beneath the pines and resumed work on his book.

Sutton and Greg rode three uneventful days into the mountains of Idaho. Other travelers gave them the news of Western Oregon's demise, the intrigue between the Federation and Deseret, and whatever rumors lingered about the power outages in the region. The pair became accustomed to the conversations and soon ignored anyone hailing them. They rode through thousands of downed timbers and pines that had been burned through in a recent wildfire. The forest cleared up and soon they came to Warm Lake. The lake had been tremendously popular up until recently. A single boat was out on the water. Scores of others were tied to a single dock or lay on their sides on the shoreline from hard weather in the spring and a jealous transient who'd pulled up their anchors and pillaged their insides. Sutton and Greg spied a pair of families camping in the campground and it was unclear to them whether this was their permanent home or not. A father stared out at the pair, holding a rifle in his hand that suggested to them they best keep moving onward.

Some distance away from the lake they came to the spot marked on their map. There was no cabin.

"Well isn't that some shit?" said Sutton.

"Fucker," muttered Greg. "He fucked us."

They dismounted and ambled around the area, looking for any indication of a cabin's prior existence. It was Sutton who found a pile of rocks at the base of a tree stump. With Greg watching on, he pulled the rocks away to reveal a hole in the stump. Within the stump was a heavy ammunition case. He opened the case and took a note from the top of an assortment of items. The note read

Hello,

There is no cabin here, as you can see. You were chosen because you provide something of value to our commune,

which lies to the east of here. Enclosed you will find a
map. You will also find one of our shielded, functioning
com-links. Please kindly remove one and leave the others
remaining for whoever makes it to this point after you.

Sutton removed one of the devices from the case, noticing there
were two others left.

The conditions of your admission to our commune are as
follows:

1. *To gain initial entry, you must tell us a story of your*
    own making when you arrive at our gates. The story
    must neither be too long, nor too short. It must be
    your own original composition. We will judge the
    merits of your story and allow you in or ask you to
    move on based on our discretion.

2. *Each member of your party must tell us a story. If*
    there were two of you when our commune member
    approached you with coordinates to the cabin near
    Warm Lake, you will each tell a story. Any additional
    members to your group since your invitation to the
    cabin will not be allowed in. We strongly urge you
    against forced entry to our commune as we are more
    than adequately equipped to repel all outsiders.

3. *Entry to the commune means a loyalty oath to its*
    secrets upon pain of death. You are allowed to leave
    the commune at any point past your probationary
    period. You are allowed to keep any and all

possessions with you upon entry. But you are not at liberty to disclose any aspect of what occurs within our wall to non-members. This is for our own protection.

4. *When your probationary period ends, you will be required to prove your loyalty to the commune during the loyalty oath ceremony. Should you prove to be disloyal during your ceremony, the punishment is death.*

5. *Agents of the Rocky Mountain Federation are not eligible for consideration.*

6. *You are being watched as we speak. We know what you look like. We know the size of your group. Should you choose not to pursue admission to our commune, we ask that you leave all contents in the case for the next applicants. If you do not, we will be forced to reclaim our property by any means necessary.*

"You're not gonna' like this," said Sutton as he held the letter in his hands.

"What is it?" asked Greg.

"Don't look around. We're being watched right now. They're probably listening, too. Here," he said as he handed the letter to his companion. "I didn't read past point six, so let me finish."

Greg took the letter, noticing its sterling letterhead immediately, and proceeded to read its contents. He muttered, "Holy hell," when he was done and handed the letter back to Sutton

7. *You were recruited to our commune for a special reason. We have abundant resources and means at our disposal. Some of our members have positions in the highest halls of power in the Rocky Mountain Federation. Our influence runs throughout much of the continent as our organization is as old as the old United States. Join us or forget you ever read this letter.*

"If they're watching us, they sure are dug in," said Sutton.

"What do you think?"

"No way in hell I'm going," was his quiet reply. "My brothers are worth more to me than anything else on this fucked up planet. I thought there'd be a cabin, we'd get fat off of fish, maybe screw some of those mountain girls Harry talked about, and end around Deseret into Nebraska. But these people are partly full of shit. There's no way the Federation would allow them into their ranks. No, they have some other means of making it out here. We should leave."

"Well then put the shit back in the case and let's get out of here before we get killed."

"Hold on."

"What are you doing?"

"Just give me a minute," said Sutton as he studied the map closely. "Okay," he said after a long few minutes. He asked Greg to remember a few details and his friend obliged him.

They rode away to the southeast in the opposite direction of where the enclosed map had said the commune would be. A drone shot out from behind a hill near where they had been reading the letter and swept in front of their faces. Both had the good sense to cover their faces with their hands. The drone followed alongside their galloping horses until Sutton leveled his pistol at it. It veered away and Sutton could see over his shoulder that it was headed back to its pilot. He and Greg rode for two hours before stopping to discuss what happened.

"They sure seemed pissed off," Sutton marveled. "A drone like that is worth a small fortune right now."

"Why did you memorize the map?" asked Greg.

"Why not? You never know when that kind of information could come in handy. I've never encountered any kind of secret society, have you? Didn't think so. Most people would give their left nut to be invited in to that kind of thing."

"Yeah, but we're not going so what's the point?"

"I was gathering intel."

"Intel? What are you going to use intel for? You're not a big shot. Your family is a bunch of orange farmers."

"Engineers and orange farmers," Sutton corrected him.

"Engineers who orange farm," Greg corrected him one further. "You and I just want to get home, hope that everyone's still alive when we get there, and get back to our old lives before the contracts. That's the deal. The cabin was going to be some fun before we got back to reality, nothing more. So, you 'gathering intel' makes me nervous, like we spent too much time with Harry and now you want to do something crazy."

"You don't think gunning down people who were trying to steal our horses in a city blown apart by nukes was crazy?"

"It was crazy enough. We're probably gonna die of cancer. What, are you gonna fly missiles into the commune when we get to Boise?"

"I'm not going to Boise," said Sutton.

"We just agreed on it!" an exasperated Greg huffed.

"I changed my mind."

"Too much time with Harry."

"Yeah, I think so."

"The sun's cooking your brain through that hat."

"Yeah, I think so," Sutton repeated with renewed emphasis.

"Okay, so you memorized the map. Now what?"

"I don't think anything. But I think we should stay away from bigger towns and cities until we're clear of Wyoming. If these people are legit, and that's a big 'if', they probably have enough people in the region to keep track of us – at least till they decide we're not a threat."

"They wanted our faces," Greg noted.

"I think they got mine."

"Me, too. We need to leave those people the fuck alone and be on with our lives."

"Gets you thinking twice about Paul?"

"Who?"

"The guy who told us about 'the cabin'," said Sutton.

"He was full of shit."

"He was probably a pedophile."

"I'm so sick of that shit," said Greg. "They're like lizards: under every rock."

"You don't want to think about it?"

"I'm exhausted. We have weeks of sleeping on the ground ahead of us with nothing to eat but some dried meat bullshit. A month ago, we had sleep monitors hooked up to us and all the pussy we could ever want."

"You knew what was coming. I thought you were ready."

"I was. I am. Goddamn, I was counting on a cabin and some fishing. I would have stayed longer at Harry's if I knew what we were going to."

"Not too late to go back," Sutton said devilishly, referring to the possibility of going to the compound with a raise of his eyebrows.

A minute passed before conversation was renewed. The surroundings were lush from unusual summer rain. Neither had been in the Sawtooth National Forest before.

"No Boise, huh?" asked Greg.

"No Boise. No Idaho Falls. No Bozeman. No Cheyenne. No nothing. They're filled with shit, anyway. How the hell do a bunch of white guys figure out how to break away from the old USA and form the same half-cocked nation they had before? Where we're from, it's better."

"They have racial quotas in Wyoming," offered Greg.

"Yeah, but the bullshit in Montana will undo all of it – that's if Deseret doesn't do it first. Who knows what's going to happen with the power grid being down or with a plague spreading everywhere?"

"Sounds like Harry changed your mind on some things."

"I'm trying it out for a change. If we can get back to Nebraska, I'm going to do things differently."

"How so?"

"I don't know yet. Maybe you, me, and my brothers can band together and take over a city hall somewhere like Harry and those guys did."

"Then what?" asked Greg, considering opening one of the packs of cigarettes Harry gifted him.

"Then we…shit, I don't know. The taxes are low, immigration is locked up tight, Northern Texas is our ally, I don't know what we'd do. It's pretty peachy back home. It took talking to Harry for two days for it to land with me."

"Why do things differently back home? Why not do them here?"

"We could ride back and track down the commune, ingratiate ourselves with them, and burn down the place in the night."

"And what if everything there is copacetic?"

"Hell, I don't know. Then we find wives and bring them home with us to Nebraska."

"I bet you that commune has something fucked up going on at it."

Sutton stopped his horse completely and considered the prospect of riding back and submitting to whoever wrote the letter in the ammunition case. Paul *seemed* normal when they talked to him in Western Oregon. If he was a pedophile, he was doing a decent job of hiding it. He had even seemed wary of the Equality Officer. There was political intrigue here he didn't understand. He wished that Harry were here to help him untangle it. Harry would know the right thing to do. He would probably encourage them to keep riding east over the endless mountains while the weather was in their favor. He would encourage them to go home to their loved ones.

"Nah, let someone else sort them out," said Sutton. "I'm surprised you'd be willing to go."

"I wasn't. I was just following your line of reasoning for a bit."

The pair made it as far as Stanley, Idaho before circumstances brought their eastward progress to a halt. A wealthy prepper with a sprawling ranch along Goat Creek beneath the towering peaks of the Sawtooth Range visited them as they were resting. He brought fishing poles, took them to the best fishing in the area, and invited them into his tremendous lodge where they soon met his family, including a stunning blonde daughter and a pretty, younger daughter. The man was severe in all matters relating to his eldest daughter. She was too beautiful for them to pass up, so they took up work on his ranch cutting hay with diesel equipment, tending to livestock, and making preparations for the eventual winter. They lived in a spare cabin. This became the respite they had hoped for with the supposed cabin at Warm Lake. The daughter, Mary Lou, took to Sutton early on more than Greg as she was compelled to the natural leadership he exhibited – reminding her of her own father. Sutton felt deep in his gut that he would not be happy with her and thus rebuffed her careful intrigue under the watchful eye of her protective father. Greg's interest grew in her over time and when Sutton made it clear to him that he would not be pursuing Mary Lou, Greg took the reins. Sutton took several hunting trips into the mountains with Lucas, the wealthy prepper, and became enamored with the Sawtooth Range.

Most of the other wealthy people in the area had not made it to their homes. Rumors had reached the ranch in Stanley that a plague was sweeping up into eastern Idaho, killing people by the tens of thousands. The prepper's hired help from out of the area had all left and none had returned, putting an impetus on Sutton and Greg to reconsider their trek down into eastern Idaho. So, they stayed into fall, Sutton going on longer and longer hunting trips with the savvy Lucas and Greg staying around the main house on the property, working slightly less every day as the chores wound down and the leaves collected on the ground. Mary Lou's younger sister pined openly for Sutton as Lucas' guard lowered but Sutton would have none of it. She was far too young and Sutton had come to feel further and further entrenched in his celibacy and general disregard for women. His experiences in Western Oregon weighed on him and sometimes when he lay awake at night, whether up in the mountains in a tent or down in the spare cabin in his own room, he would think about violence toward the urbane women of Portland. In his heart, it wasn't enough for him that they were likely all dead. He wanted his revenge. The resentment smoldered in him and he kept away from Greg and Mary Lou whenever they were together.

Greg, on the other hand, had not felt the ideological spark from their short, intense stay with Harry. He was less intellectually inclined than Sutton. He cared not for the wider political intrigue, who did what and why it mattered when. The long journey through eastern Oregon and Idaho had put him squarely focused on fertility. Wherever they had gone, they had either been leered at with murderous suspicion or heard stories of families torn apart by violence, tribal clashes between racial groups, or the swarm-like tendencies of Deseret and its ambitions for what lay north. Greg wanted a wife and children. Mary Lou was his best bet. Lucas was approving and so the relationship was accepted on the ranch.

Mary Lou was 19 years old. She was one of the 'mountain girls' Harry had told Sutton and Greg about. She had spent her whole life in Stanley. When the political climate of the times finally made its way to Boise, her father took her and her two younger sisters down through Sun Valley into eastern Idaho and sometimes all the way to Salt Lake City. The political winds shifted and soon it was the Ketchum and Sun Valley path that was closed off to them. With the power grid going down, as Lucas had anticipated, the few families left in Stanley shifted into their self-sufficient gear. Mary Lou carried on as if nothing was different. Her mother, Lucas' second wife, had been sex-trafficked as a teenager. As a result, she put into Mary Lou a strong suspicion of society. She'd taught her daughter there were few strong, decent men left in the world – her father being one of them. Mary Lou was only to trust men of her own race who reminded her of her father: tall, intelligent, sturdy, and willing to protect their loved ones at all costs. Lucas' initial suspicions of Sutton and Greg work as breeders in the debauchery capital of the continent was allayed when they shared stories of their former lives in Nebraska and what they had done since journeying east. If Lucas was allayed, then Mary Lou was allayed.

She relaxed and let her personality show. She was sweet when Greg came calling after the day's work but reserved when he strayed into the intellectual, forgetting her inexperience and distaste for the wider world. She was dutiful to her parents to a fault. Sometimes her mother had nightmares. She would check on her mother in the night. Her mother moaned aloud memories of torture when Lucas was away, taking his turn at the village guard post along the highway. Greg got more of the backstory on her mother, bit by bit as Mary Lou felt she could trust him. Through the summer and partway into the fall there was no physical contact in their courtship. Mary Lou wouldn't allow it. Nor would her parents but they had receded some, seeing how aloof Sutton had become. They hoped they weren't pushing him away but their stoic nature kept them from bringing it up. They didn't want to scare away such a compatible suitor as Greg, even if their daughter was a bit young to be considering marriage.

Sutton discovered Lucas' library. It was in the airplane hangar on the property. He mentioned to Lucas the rows of bookcases lining the second story platform built into the inner corner of the hangar. Lucas gave him permission to read any book he pleased so long as he promised to keep the books in the condition they were in. Sutton's brief time with Harry had left an indelible impact on him. Harry was so much more a vocal man than Sutton's father was. The wide-ranging intellectual curiosity of a person so well versed in the political and philosophical climate of a Western world at war with itself went from a novelty to Sutton to a way of living. He dove headfirst into a rigorous study of Lucas' 20,000 book library. He paused only to do work on the ranch or hunt in the mountains. These breaks permitted him time to assimilate. Soon he was taking the more beat up paperbacks he could muster out into the mountains with him. He found he could read three or four books in a week. He discovered self-knowledge. He learned that men had spent whole days debating one another to captivated audiences capable of hours and hours of devoted concentration. This intelligence he'd been engineered to have was useful beyond outperforming his brothers and contributing genetic material to the witch queens of Western Oregon. His knowledge of what he could do with his intelligence was made known to him from the limited selection of books on intelligence research Lucas possessed. He tore through those books in a week and spent the better part of an afternoon combing over the remainder of the library in the hopes of finding further readings on the subject.

On the day of the first snow of the season, Greg and Mary Lou were riding horses through tall pines at the foot of the mountains. Mary Lou's beautiful blonde hair was tied back in a long braid. Greg leaned over, flicked it, and smiled warmly when she gave him a look.

"I love you," he told her for the first time.

She blushed and said the same in return.

They kissed passionately when they returned to the horse barn. The snow outside was mixed with rain. A light breeze blew through the barn, scattering hay in its wake. Greg laughed to himself as he left the barn with Mary Lou, one hand wrapped around her svelte waist. Sutton would be happy for his friend but also disappointed as all signs pointed to Greg staying at Lucas' ranch and marrying Mary Lou there. Only a woman of

Mary Lou's caliber could have wrenched Greg away from Sutton and the journey home. Just as Liam had stayed behind for a woman, so would Greg. The possibility had not been lost on Sutton. They spoke that night by their cabin's stone fireplace.

Greg sat down at a leather chair near Sutton and said, "I'm in love with her."

"I guess you'll be staying then," said Sutton, looking up from his book with a smile.

"You're not?"

"I'll stay, at least through spring. Too much to learn here and I may not get a second chance."

"Why care to learn? The world's gone to shit. Pedophiles run everything and the few free places left keep losing territory. Where's the room for caring in a world of violence?"

"I don't know," said Sutton, setting his book down in earnest and giving his friend his full attention. "How do you know it's love? She's about as good looking as they get. Why not lust?"

"She's a good person, that's how I know it's love."

"Not like you could have screwed her if you wanted. Well, I guess you get to now," he ribbed his friend.

"Hadn't thought of it much."

"Come on, with as good a-lookin' as she is?"

"You sound more like Harry every day," was Greg's retort. "She was yours if you wanted her."

"She's yours and you're staying. That's for the best. I'll stay cause we're just getting to the good part of the year where I get to read as many books as I can."

"I don't think they do you as good as you think."

"Why's that?"

"You get anxious for a world that doesn't exist, a time that never was. Civilization has fallen. The best you can hope for yourself is to find love, have as many kids as you can feed, and hole up somewhere until things get better."

"How are things going to get better?"

"The bad guys will wear themselves out," said Greg. "Something will give and people will come together again."

"I don't think the bad guys will wear themselves out. I think they need killing."

"Like we did in Portland?"

"No, not like that. Like those people who tried recruiting us in the summer, the ones who put a drone on us."

"You're still thinking about that?"

"Now and then."

"You want me and Lucas to saddle up with you and go find them?"

"It's a thought. Not with winter setting in like this, though. We'll be up to our asses in snow in a couple weeks. Besides, there's not enough of us."

"Then what's the point in putting in the study like this?"

"Makes me more aware. It gives me purpose. I learn what I didn't know."

"Then what are you going to put it to use for?"

"I don't know, Greg. I just know I need to do it. Reading these books give me resolve, like I'll know the right thing to do when my moment comes."

"The world is emptying out. I'm glad you have something that gives you meaning."

"It'd give you meaning, too."

"Yeah, probably. But I'm busy right now."

"Her head's fuller than yours, that's why it's gratifying," said Sutton.

"You think so?"

"Absolutely. She's read some of the older books in the hangar. Her mother classically educated her. She's just bashful about it. Probably doesn't want you to know what she's like underneath the reluctance. That's my hunch."

"How do I figure that out?"

"You have to do the work yourself. Your parents raised you to fuck around and get a cushy job when you calmed down."

"That's not fair," said Greg.

"It's the truth."

"Well, you just started with all these books. That's not how you grew up."

"That's fair. But I was raised to think independently. That was my foundation."

"You think that's what the world needs?"

Sutton considered the question, resting in his chair and watching the fire in the fireplace. He looked up at the large beams spanning the ceiling and said, "No," with a strained voice, "I think the world needs moral justice. Thinking independently is the foundation of that. I think the world needs some of what Harry was talking about. He had a lot of the right answers, he just didn't talk about how to get to them. I'm getting to them now. The world needs moral justice...and intelligence. Only the intelligent should be allowed to breed. But that's not good enough. They have to prove that somehow they are upstanding people, that they won't use their intelligence for evil…and how you impose those conditions without ensuring that evil people eventually corrupt the institutions upholding the conditions, I don't know."

"There are no institutions left. This is all hypothetical."

"Do you feel yourself thinking?" asked Sutton with a wry smile.

"You turn more and more into him every day," Greg referred to Harry.

"No, I'm my own guy. I won't fail my family."

"You think that's what he did? To me it was more like society corrupted his family and turned them against him. If he failed, it was that he didn't live near them."

"No, he failed them. That's why he's alone. Why else would he be alone like that?"

"I thought it was because he was a crank."

"A crank? That guy is kind as could be. He is haunted."

"He sure was unhappy about the world."

"That's true," said Sutton.

"How do you figure he failed his family?"

"He knew the illness but he didn't know the cure. The illness will spread here, too, if you don't know what to do about it."

"This is paradise. There's no way. The people here have this valley locked down."

"Maybe. But I think the men here know what the illness is and they've inoculated their families against it. Do you see how everyone here is kind but protective as hell? Up here in the mountains everyone asks us to show them our chests to see if we've pledged allegiance to enemy nations or not. Everyone who submits to evil has some kind of permanent marker on them, even if it's just spiritual. If you don't give in to the mark, the evil people eventually mass on your border and then overwhelm you when they have enough numbers. You have to always look out for the mark of evil and kill anyone who carries it before they can plot against you."

"This sounds like something from the Bible," observed Greg. "This is your answer to what has happened out there?"

"I'd say it's the blueprint. But you have to have the moral courage to see it through."

"So, stupid people don't get to breed? That's part of your blueprint?"

"I don't know. I don't think they should but they also can't help being born stupid. I think it would hurt the good people to start imposing those rules on people. I'm just working this stuff out in my head."

"You're going to restart civilization? That's a hell of a difference from when we first came here!"

"No, I don't think that's possible. I'm tempted to stay here with you as long as possible, just study for like 5 years. Mary Lou's a catch. I was stupid to turn her away."

"She's got a sister…"

"Her sister's not as smart as her. I want a smart one. I have enough time."

"You never know when you'll catch a bullet," said Greg. "Especially if you're raiding communes and reordering society as you see fit. She's got a sister…" he repeated in a singsong voice.

"You know, I haven't jerked off in two months. It's true. For all that puss we caught in Portland…two months. It's liberating. We were paid a fortune to stick our dicks into machines and get milked. What a nightmare. Two months."

"I'm on a month without jerking off. Two months is good, brother. How long you think it'll take before we get all of that shit out of our heads?"

"Another couple years. Walks in the Sawtooth help me."

"I sit in the creek. It's nice and cold."

"Have you done anything with Mary Lou?"

"No, she won't let me. She says she's saving herself for her wedding night and it's non-negotiable. I respect it. Something about it feels clean, like respecting her this way is cleansing to me."

"It is. I won't do it again outside of marriage."

"Really! You *have* changed. Pietro would be choking you out right now, slapping you in the face and shit."

They both laughed at the bittersweet memory of their friend. They began talking about the man's wild antics. Pietro would rebel against their situation by openly masturbating in front of a matriarch whenever he could get one alone. They would shriek and run away but as the only misbehavior clause in his breeder contract involved violent crime or fraud, he couldn't be removed from his position. He also thought it was hilarious to cross-dress and sneak into female-only establishments, which by law comprised 51% of establishments in Portland. He would defecate in the most difficult to clean places that he could find. Female-only establishments had to hire female-only staff, including janitorial services, and Pietro loved the dark comedy of his revenge on women. One time, on a dare, he walked into the city courthouse, went straight into the office of a city commissioner (all of them being matriarchs), sat on her lap and burped in her face as loudly as he could. He spent the next ten minutes sprinting around city hall, evading capture by equality officers before being tased into submission. His deviltry didn't end at this point however as he had purposely not peed in several hours and proceeded to pee his pants as he was carried away by the steroid-enhanced officers. The punishment for his various rebellions always involved humiliating punishment by the soccer players during workouts, thus further fueling his resentment. Breeders were part of the elite class in the small coastal country that were not subject to laws for regular citizens. Pietro abused this privilege at least a few times a month.

When their reminiscences subsided, they sat quietly in their sadness. Sutton's inquiries were opening up an emotional distance between them. Greg was nowhere near as interested in these philosophical questions. Part of it was an intellectual defense: a need to defend his adherence to a life in Stanley that was, by most means, superior to what he could be returning to in Nebraska. Part of it was that it was Greg's disposition to be steady and strong for those around him without offering intellectual leadership. He didn't want that role. His personality wasn't suited for it, he'd decided. And what Sutton was hinting at would take him away from Mary Lou. He was tortured about the developing distance. He had the courage to go with Sutton but knew that Sutton didn't require it of him. Sutton didn't need him as a soulmate. Their paths would eventually part. Neither thought it would happen so soon. Perhaps it wouldn't. Perhaps Sutton would be content to continue his studies as he professed he would. The very fact that he spoke this way gave Greg the distinct sense that he was a man itching for trouble or for action of some kind. When Sutton wasn't working, reading, or up in the mountains, he was pacing in the hangar – mulling things over. Greg would pretend not to see him through the bay windows when he was off to somewhere with Mary Lou.

Winter was long and filled with more of the same for the two men. Their host tried from time to time to encourage Sutton toward his second eldest daughter to no avail. Sutton was a man possessed in his studies. Nothing would deny him his awakening. The dead of winter reduced his chores to firewood and brief forays into the greenhouse. Village duties were closed down as the snow was too heavy and nobody needed to patrol for outsiders. It was in the silence of the falling snow and beneath a towering cottonwood tree that Greg proposed to Mary Lou. They agreed to marry the first week of spring. The village's lone deacon agreed to marry them at the town's chapel, formerly a meditation center before all leftists were run out of town twenty years prior. The wedding came and went in late May. Sutton dropped a few hints that wherever he went and whoever he found, he would perhaps return to Stanley to raise a family. Lucas' patronage and willingness to share his 80-acre ranch with people of "good moral fiber" was the main draw. Sutton talked of his brothers longingly only when he became restless and overwhelmed from the books he was reading. He spoke to Greg about the majesty of the Sawtooth Range in terms that gave the impression he was home. Nor was his lingering focus entirely auto-derived.

Lucas, his wife, and the few friends they had in the area were apprehensive and hopeful that he would stay. Greg would make a good steward of the ranch when Lucas was too old to be at the helm but privately, Lucas wished for Sutton's leadership. Sutton had a timeless, human quality to him – a nobility and innocence that garnered confidence among only the most perceptive. Greg was more apparently dutiful and hard working. Sutton, however, had an aspect to him that glimmered the promise of true greatness. He had little grasp of it and sometimes, for weeks, it would go underground. But Lucas saw it in him. This part of Sutton reminded him of a heroic general Lucas had served under when the original American nation was tearing apart. The general had made Lucas' fortune and the fortune of many other patrons who settled in the Rockies to escape the roving massacres and famines that tore through the rest of the continent. The solemn retreat of these men and above all, their leader, put into context what Sutton was doing now. Sutton's patrimony was Lucas' estate, he was sure of it. He was sure of it when he would see Sutton walk to the storehouse to withdraw another pack of the endless candles contained there so he could read later into the night. He was sure of it when he saw how Sutton worked with the cattle and their calving season, which had begun in the middle of a snowstorm. He saw it in the fidelity of Greg's eyes when Sutton philosophized about the mistakes of the modern world over a dinner with the clan. Just as Lucas' general had, Sutton belonged to the line of rare white men who charted the course for the rest.

Sutton didn't want the ranch, not yet anyway. Before the spring was done, Lucas granted him leave to go and visit Harry. Sutton rode down through Lowman and across the plains of western Idaho – doing his best to avoid contact with others. He noted how fewer people there were out and about, compared to the year before. He thought of the commune north of Warm Lake but his eagerness to speak with Harry put the thought out of his head before long. After a week of hard riding split by a day's rest in the middle, he arrived at the log arch of Harry's place. Harry's faithful cattle dog sprinted out to meet him. Sutton shot up the private road that wound through trees to Harry's cabin, nestled in a copse of pine and spruce. The trees had been meticulously planted by the previous owner long ago.

"You look redder than a beet!" exclaimed Harry as he set his rifle against a log column supporting the awning over his weathered deck.

"Oh yeah, there's no damn cover from here to where I'm living."

"Where's that, then?"

"A ranch in Stanley."

"Big money, huh? I'm surprised you settled so close to Sun Valley."

"I think those are just rumors. That's what the guy I'm living with says."

"Maybe, maybe. And Greg? How's he holding up?"

"Just fine. Got himself a woman: our boss' daughter. He married her a few weeks ago."

Harry helped Sutton unpack his horse and set it loose in a small fenced pasture. He fixed them up lunch while Sutton played with the dog and toured the property for any changes Harry had made in the previous year. A few sheds were repainted and the irrigation line was diverted so Harry could collect water into a pool for his horses. Harry brought him a plate with tinned meat, potato chips, and pickles on it as he stood watching the water flow into the pool.

"See that real green patch over there?" Harry asked and pointed. "The pool drains into that somehow. I think it's the clay in the soil that moves the water there. It's a veritable oasis. Almost as good as the spring."

"Why the pool?" asked Sutton.

"Oh, the next guy down the line moved out. In the bylaws you're allowed to build one if that's the case."

"I'm surprised the irrigation is coming through."

"Well, we're not fucked yet," chuckled Harry. "Come on, let's get in the shade." When they were situated and eating their lunches, Harry asked, "What brings you out here?"

"I have a decision to make. You're the wisest person I know."

"Oh, I'm not wise. Just long in the tooth. If I were wise, I'd have a lot more people around me to take care of me as my joints turn to a fine powder and my back decides it's one of these," he held up the potato chip in his hand before biting down on it loudly for effect. "What's your decision?"

"I have three choices, as I can see it. I can stay where I'm at with Greg since he's settling in Stanley. The guy that owns the ranch wants to give it to me when he turns 65, which is in ten years. I can keep moving east, probably at the end of the summer, and go back home to Nebraska."

"Wait, you were headed for a cabin at Warm Lake. What happened to that?"

"That's the third option. There wasn't a cabin. There was a lockbox with an invitation to a commune north of there. They wanted a loyalty oath and said they had secrets, so we moved on. But I have the map to their commune charted out from memory. The way they worded it was that if you go, you're either in or you die."

"Probably pedophiles…"

"That's what I thought. It's been gnawing at me. What if it's not?"

"They wouldn't be so pushy up front if they weren't hiding something. Probably Jews or pedophiles or some rich dude who managed to get ahold of a nuke."

"You haven't heard anything?"

"The only thing I've heard is that a fair number of people are dying off around here from the lack of medical care. Anyone who had diabetes is basically gone. That's all I've heard. Haven't seen the Bridger folks in a couple months. Word gets around slower and slower."

"I should probably leave that one out, then."

"Anyone who wants a blood oath from you is up to no good. Blood oaths are unchristian and you don't need that kind of trouble. You're too smart to need them for anything. Look how you've managed for yourself. How big is the ranch?"

"80 acres."

"Outside the valley or in it?"

"In it."

Harry set his plate down and raised his eyebrows in surprise at Sutton, "That's prime real estate. Places like that only go for sale, or least they did, once every ten years. That's almost like one of those island homes on Flathead Lake that people hold onto for grim death. Prime real estate. I live in the shit sticks compared to that."

"You could come to Stanley with me…"

"I could," mused Harry. "Let me think on it."

"I'd be more inclined to stay there if you did."

"Why?"

"I've been thinking about it. I don't think my family needs me in Nebraska."

"Nonsense. You're as good as they get, kid. Why wouldn't they need you?"

"Why didn't they say anything when I took the contract as a breeder? They just wished me well and watched me go off to hell."

Harry picked up a bit of tinned meat from his plate and uttered, "Oh, boy," before taking tossing the bit to his dog. "That's a hell of an angle. You think that's worth giving up on them over."

"The way I see is that they gave on me."

"Oofta," Harry exhaled. "I have a hard time seeing it."

"You gave up on your family."

"Oofta, don't do that to me, Sutton. I don't want to think about it."

"Do you deny it?"

"I didn't know I was gonna' be on trial at my own place. Shit, I'm sorry. You're just throwing me for a hell of a curve right now. I'm dizzy. Hold on, let me think."

They sat in silence. Harry would come out of his reverie to eat a little or pet his dog. Sutton had the distinct sense that he needed to remain patient, otherwise he would throw Harry off track and Harry would deflect again.

Finally, when his food was gone, Harry spoke again, "I could have done more. I've probably said as much but it was always to get sympathy for myself. The way you're putting it to me, I can see you're recruiting me. But you want to be sure I don't give up on you. What the hell are you up to over there, Sutton?"

"I don't know what I'm up to."

"Something's brewing, though. I can see that. I own it. I gave up on my family. You're not giving up on yours. They gave up on you. You could have turned into a faggot with all that porn, casual pussy, and feminism they were pumping you full of. They left you to rot."

"I'm still considering going back, though."

"Why?"

"My brothers weren't all bad. They have some of the same problems I do."

"But they didn't say anything…"

"No, they didn't."

"And you're the youngest, aren't you?"

"Yeah."

"Then it was their job to protect you. I'm just following the logic here."

"I know, it's why I came. It's not like I could have called you or dropped a line."

"I'm honored, son."

It was Sutton's turn to deflect. He stood up and said, "I need to take a shit. Your toilet still working?" He went into the cabin and sat on the toilet, noticing that Harry had changed the magazines on the rack against the wall. He chuckled at the man's conscientiousness. He had come to Harry looking for clarity and he'd gotten it straight away. The truth was that he had fallen in love with the West and was looking to reinforce his position. He wouldn't admit this to himself. He couldn't, at least until this moment.

Part Three

Harry agreed to join Sutton at the ranch in Stanley. They stayed at his cabin for a week, packing what needed to be packed onto several horses. The place was turned over for safekeeping to the Bridger outfit. They could use the place as they saw fit so long as they didn't build near the cabin.

Nearly a week into their trip eastward to Stanley, they were traveling on a highway winding through dried up hills and mountains looming in the background. A shot rang out, whizzing just above Harry's head. Both men dropped from their horses, Harry cursing at the pain in his feet from landing on the asphalt awkwardly. A second shot rang out not long after, telling them it was probably only one person with a bolt action rifle. Harry's dog sprinted to the edge of the river by the side of the highway and barked in the direction of the rifle fire. A third shot rang out, grazing the flank of one of Harry's horses. Sutton and Harry caught the muzzle flash and unloaded their rifles into the thicket from which it came. No further fire came. Sutton chased down the one horse that had been spooked by the gunfire. It was a two-year old that was still learning to carry a saddle and wasn't accustomed to Harry's target practice at his place like the others were. Harry waded into the river, his rifle affixed on the source of the fire. His dog was just barely tall enough to accompany him. Harry scampered up the hill to the thicket of trees as quickly as his old legs would take him, his dog already on site and sniffing a dead body. Sutton joined them a moment later.

"Looks like you got him," Harry moved the shooter's head to the side, revealing the large entry wound and the carnage of what had once been the back of the man's skull. Sutton's was the rifle capable of this level of damage.

Sutton exhaled through his nose and shook his head in disgust. He looked at the man's face, unable to decide if he was American Native or Hispanic. The man was clearly starving to death, explaining his errant shots and lazy ambush. Further inspection of the area revealed a shoddy campsite, some fishing gear, and a revolting ditch filled with rusting cans and open sewage.

"What the hell was he thinking?" asked Sutton, heavy with confusion and dismay.

"He wasn't thinking. Look at all this. He was living like an animal."

"How the hell did he make it this far north with as little as he had?"

"It's not our place to care and you know the answer, anyway. Come on, kid," said Harry. He whistled for his dog. They crossed back over the river. Sutton suggested they dig a grave for the shooter but Harry waved him off, stating the shooter would not have done the same for him. "Reciprocity is everything anymore," he added with finality. They continued on their way, on high alert for the rest of the day. When night was falling and they came to a rare intersection along the way, they encountered a large family traveling as a caravan. They confirmed with Harry the danger of passage through Hells Canyon on the way up to Elk City, where their family owned a cabin redoubt. The patriarch of the family hardened his face at the news and the prospect of what would be a difficult final leg of their trip. He bid Sutton and Harry on their way but not before giving them the news that indeed the power had gone out through all of the Federation. Much of Idaho was still navigable. This was remarkable in that most places across the continent would explode into pandemonium within a week of essential services being cut off.

Sutton and Harry were having their first discussion of the day on the home stretch into the Stanley Basin past one of the village's three entry checkpoints.

"I've killed three people now," said Sutton. "All of them in the past year."

"Those killings were in self-defense," Harry offered. "You'll probably kill a few more, the way things are looking. I've only killed the one but I think my count will go up. We're small time compared to what the Deseret elders did. They ran poison through their water treatment plants. They were systematic about it, too. Kept their favored wards alive. That's why they're so desperate to recruit now. It wasn't the murderous pack of thieves running Denver like they said it was. And that's nothing compared to the wars. Too many ways of killing people nowadays. Killing in self-defense is damn near a noble act these days. You know they used to make movies about violent anarchy back in the day. Oh yeah, anarcho-tyranny," he said with special emphasis to familiarize Sutton with the term. "What we have today was imagined up by techno-pedophiles and put into movies by whatever talent they could siphon up into their hierarchies. It was a mad grab for money, property, and fame before the waves of violence hit. They knew it was coming and they put a marketing spin on everything. Anybody under a certain intelligence simply does as they're programmed, so they made sure they weren't the antagonists in their own films. There's something Darwinian about it: programming low IQ people to kill other low IQ people. What we have now was planned a long time ago. It's the best cover for getting away with what they're doing to children now. You cloak the civilized world in pandemonium so no one faction is strong enough to break your trafficking networks or turn back your kidnapping squads. The whole while you're blasting the general public with programming nudging them toward their own demise. You think all these nations that rose up in the past twenty years are free and clear? You're from the best one, the only one with a decent immigration policy, and you still let anyone vote. Whites are still getting outbred so it's only a matter of time before the ones you didn't deport will outnumber you. Here in the Federation we only get by because nobody wants to live out here since there's no jobs, no welfare, and apparently, no power grid either."

"Greg says all you can do is have a family and hunker down to wait it out."

"I think so. I think that's all you can do. You can try to keep our Western traditions alive," he said as he patted the saddlebag containing one of his printed manuscripts and several copies of another book he self-published.

"Why not kill the real bad guys? The ones running everything into the ground."

"The Christian Knights did a bit of that. You could get a bit of momentum in that direction, even despite the media lying about everything you were doing, but they would root you out with the 'cyber-security' that is their god. Next thing you know, you're getting strangled to death in your jail cell while the security cameras are experiencing a malfunction and they string your dead body up with a bed sheet to make it look like you killed yourself. By the time a sizeable enough contingent of people got wise to this, it was already too late and the Satan-worshippers could put any politician into power that they wanted. The original United States broke up when they passed a Federal firearm ban that targeted anyone who'd ever said anything in support or in sympathy with the Christian Knights. The pedophiles activated all their deep state sleeper cells and started killing all their enemies outright. They'd pose as police come to take your firearms. The Internet was completely censored at that point. Then the panics happened and so on and so forth."

"There's no cyber-security now."

"There isn't, as far as we know."

"That means the pedophiles are isolated from each other. Some of those EMP's must have been in self-protection by somebody. No electronics, no infiltration and brainwashing."

"Yeah, but it means no medical equipment or transportation." Harry laughed and corrected himself, "But what's worse? Pedophiles run amuck with their digital god or not being able to get an MRI? If mankind can't play nice, someone has to take the toys away. Someone just put America in timeout."

"Or it just happened by coincidence out of the sheer chaos. I don't think the secret societies are as strong as they were. There's no central marketplace or bank to pilfer from because there hasn't been enough trust that your money won't just be put to use against you by some piece of shit Third Worlder or secret society pedophile at the next possible juncture."

"I hadn't thought of it that way. Son, you've been hitting the books."

"With the power grid down and the digital networks dead, they can't enforce the laws requiring you to participate.

Participation is gone, completely. And only in the past year. Parasites don't squirrel away for winter…"

"Some of them do."

"Some of them do," repeated Sutton. "But how sustainable is a life of bringing kids to you so you can rape them, when all the technology is down? They have to come out of their hiding holes and do some of their dirty work themselves now. Or sustain the children they have on hand until the lights come back on. That's not exactly their wheelhouse. Left here. It's at the end of the road."

"Damn, that's something. How many houses are there on the ranch?"

"Six total. Three are empty because the hired help cleared out last year. Only a couple people stayed. They stay in that cabin at the edge of the hill there. I live in the cabin there by the pond. The big boss lives in that one, obviously. That's it. He'll be happy to have you and no offense, especially the dog."

"None taken. There he is!" Harry cried out upon seeing Greg. His dog was already sprinting ahead to greet Greg. The man walked hurriedly, pausing for just a moment to acknowledge the dog. He gave a thin smile to the older man and his friend but his eyes were tired and troubled.

"There's a man here," he said and watched the men's hands go to their sidearms. "No, he's fine. It's Kevin Tedrick."

"The movie star?" said Harry, full of surprise.

"The one and only. He's hurt. Shot through the stomach and a couple other places. Come on."

They hurried to the horse barn, unburdened their animals, and made directly for the lodge where Kevin was being treated by the lone medically capable person in Stanley, a retired nurse practitioner from the defunct Salmon River Clinic who was slowly dying of cancer. They arrived as she was closing the pine door with a frosted glass window that just barely revealed a tall figure propped up on a bed.

"These are Sutton and Harry," Greg introduced them to Cassie Marshall.

Cassie greeted them and told them she'd given Kevin a sedative and assured them he would live, that his fever had already broken. The man needed his rest. Lucas arrived, his arms coated in blood – most of it dried. He nodded his greeting to Harry and asked the men for help in salvaging what meat they could from Kevin's dead horse. They left Cassie and her charge to go to the second horse barn where Harry's dog was already pawing at the stall where the horse had just died from its wounds. It was a magnificent blonde horse that Kevin had spent a small fortune on a decade prior. In a few pained words, he had already given his permission to Lucas to do what was needed with the horse should it die.

"What a crying shame," said Lucas as he brought meat to his wife and a neighbor woman to can and smoke. The ranch dogs were busy making quick work of what meat had been considered ruined. Lucas turned his attention back to the bloody mess of the horse carcass. He showed Sutton how to strip the meat from the bones most efficiently after instructing Greg to show Harry to his new quarters in one of the unused cabins. They parted to carry Harry's many saddlebags of varying sizes and materials into his new home.

Evening came after a long day of hard work and Kevin Tedrick was feeling well enough to have visitors. Sutton accompanied Lucas to Kevin's room.

"I appreciate you putting me up," said Kevin to Lucas as they entered and sat at the chairs Cassie had brought in.

"It's the least I could do," offered Lucas.

"My horse?"

Lucas shook his head. Kevin winced. He buried his face into his hands and after a few seconds he returned his gaze to his visitors, a single tear falling from his eye. He spoke in a quieter voice, "Your family will be well-fed for a while. I don't want any of it. That's too much."

Lucas stepped out to confer with Cassie and ensure the broth being prepared for Kevin would be free of his horse. Sutton remained, unsure of what to say to a man he'd seen only on movie posters.

"What's your name?" Kevin asked him.

"Sutton."

"That's your name? That's a last name. What's your first name?"

"That's my first name. My last name is Reese."

"Hell of a name. I'm Kevin Tedrick."

"You used to be in the movies."

"Just a bit. They ran me out."

"The pedophiles?"

"Basically. None of the online studios would take me, either."

"You did a few Christian movies, right?"

"Just a few. The magic wasn't in it, so I retired to Montana when the wars opened up."

"How'd you end up here?" Sutton asked him as Lucas reentered the room.

"That'd be the question, wouldn't it? Where to start. We formed an outfit a month ago up in Montana. We went and killed some satanics that had a compound north of us. Our numbers grew so we came down to Sun Valley, well northwest of it by a ways. Probably only a half hour in a car, though. These satanics were a lot more prepared. We got scattered. I went west, where I thought a couple of my best guys had made out to. Two of the compound guards caught up to me and put a few bullets in me before I shot them dead. Yours was the first place that let me in."

"How many men were with you?" asked Lucas.

"Twelve others. We did a recon of the place for two days and only saw ten people, including a few of their elite. You know, the ones that have had all the surgeries. We engaged, another twenty or thirty poured out of the place, we couldn't get a foothold, and we broke off. I saw three of my guys shot dead. I would have thought I'd have seen the pair that came out this way by now. The good bit of it is our jamming drone was working when we tore out of there. The guy running it, Russell, is tough as nails. But who knows. We all agreed if we were overwhelmed, everyone would do their best to confuse any pursuers before backtracking to Montana."

"Cassie says you've got a month before you can ride again, three weeks if you push it. She said you're real lucky."

"Greg and I can go look for your friends," said Sutton.

With a harsh knock at the door, Lucas' wife peered her head through and said to Lucas that two people had come to the ranch and were waiting outside. Kevin gave him a look that said to be careful as he motioned for Sutton to come with him. Lucas went to his study with Sutton in tow and withdrew two 1911 style pistols from a heavy vault built into a stone accent wall. He nodded to Sutton as he put a pistol into the back of his belt and handed Sutton the other. They walked to the large double front doors into the main lodge and stepped out to see a man and a woman-to-man mounted on horses wearing all black, including thick sunglasses.

"You're the owner?" asked the woman-to-man.

"That'd be me," was all Lucas said. Without moving his gaze, he noticed Harry and Greg step out quietly onto the balcony affixed to the side of the hangar. They were armed with rifles that they carefully obscured from sight as they crouched down to where they could not be seen by the intruders. Darkness was falling and the solar powered light system switched on, illuminating the faces of the guards who had come to the property.

"We're looking for a murderer who may have passed through here. He is wanted in Ketchum for an assault he and others carried out on the municipal government. We have apprehended one of his accomplices, who died in our custody last night from wounds sustained during the attack. Have you seen anyone come into the valley here?"

"People come and go through here but nobody in the last day. What'd he look like?"

"One of our people he shot says he has sandy brown hair, has a large nose, is tall, and handsome. The person he shot is now dead. This man is a murderer and the Town of Ketchum is offering working electronics, munitions, and gold for his capture. We believe he may be the leader of the bandits that attacked our government center," said the man in black. He scanned his eyes around the ranch greedily.

Up on the hangar balcony, Greg and Harry were whispering to each other.

"I'll take the long-haired one, you take the other," said Greg, loading rounds into the Henry rifle available to him when the intruders made their appearance.

"Easy, son. They don't know we're here. That's to our advantage."

Harry wiped the sweat from his brow and sighed heavily to relieve his elevated heart rate. He watched Greg continue to load the rifle and close the magazine tube discreetly. He looked back to the interaction that was playing out.

Lucas spoke curtly to the Ketchum guards, "Your presence here breaks the agreement between our towns."

"We are aware," said the male. He telegraphed his motion to throw a small leather bag of silver to Lucas and then did so. "With the Salmon River power situation, there may be some reconsideration of the agreement between our towns. Our offer on the fugitive is a side issue. We have deep coffers. He is more valuable to us alive. We appreciate your time."

Lucas tossed the silver back to the male. The pair in black turned and rode off at a gallop. Everyone on the ranch breathed a sigh of relief. Kevin Tedrick watched from a window, grimacing at the thought of the scrutiny he had brought the ranch under.

Sutton and Lucas returned to his room still carrying their weapons.

"What do you think?" Lucas asked Kevin.

Kevin pondered the question for a long while, much in the same manner Sutton was given to. His countenance was not lost on the young man, who already worshipped the grizzled actor. "I don't know. They don't have the tech. We disabled a lot of it in the firefight. If they come back, they'll come back in numbers. Nobody in their town cares for them, that much is clear."

"They never do," said Lucas.

"They may not come back. You giving back the money may have tipped them off."

"Shit, I know."

"Why don't we take the fight to them?" asked Sutton. "If they lost their tech, we could pick them off from a distance."

Lucas waved off the suggestion. Kevin hobbled back to the window and brooded. His thick fingers scratched at his beard. He thought of his son and his wife at the cabin near North Fork. He wondered if Terry and Sue had followed them there. "Your town guard didn't stop them," he noted.

"The promise of working electronics is about as persuasive as it gets right now," said Lucas. "The Salmon River Co-op is defunct. Deseret don't come this far north. Some people feel stranded but they don't want to live under the compound's rules in Ketchum."

"How many men can we count on here?" Kevin asked.

"There's…five of us here and two neighbors I'd trust with my life," said Lucas. "The village has got a fair number of big money loner types. They won't fight for anything except themselves but they won't bother us either."

"The town guard?"

"It rotates. Today it was the Hammond twins. They're poor shots. Shopkeepers. They're corruptible but they don't have the balls to come at us by joining up with the enemy."

"You ex-military?" Kevin asked Lucas.

"Yup."

"What about you?" Kevin put the question to Sutton.

"He's not," Lucas replied. "I've been teaching him to shoot on hunts. He's damn good."

"If I leave, you'll be safe."

"Nonsense. If you killed Satanists, we stand with you. If they come back, we'll kill them. Every single one of them."

"My son in North Fork has automatic rifles," said Kevin. "My men will be there."

"We have plenty of rifles here. Grenades, claymores, two RPG's, and a few other things. Everybody's trained, even my daughters."

"It's a mad world."

"It sure is. You need your rest. You'll be wanting to get back to your people as soon as possible, I'd imagine."

Kevin gave a quick nod that signified he was done talking for the time being.

Kevin was quick to recover, far ahead of the timetable Cassie Marshall had set for him. Lucas paid her well in food and new clothing so that she would maintain silence about Kevin's presence on the ranch. She was the only person outside of the ranch who knew he was in Stanley, as he had ridden in under the cover of darkness. Under ordinary circumstances, the presence of the last Western film stars would have stirred a hubbub of excitement and gossip as cowboy culture was still in fashion in the area. Since the mail service had gone down, a bolo tie and hatmaker from Challis had started making his rounds through the various towns in the Sawtooth National Forest. He carted along with him any cowboy boots he could resole in his amateur fashion and resell. The few girls in Stanley, Lucas' daughters included, wore woolen gored skirts. Some of the women made silken hitched skirts that were worn for special occasions such as weddings and the two annual fairs that had ceased the year prior.

Despite Kevin's anxiety to get going on his way and reunite with his family, Sutton and Kevin struck up an easy friendship. Sutton asked plenty of questions, Kevin gave simple replies. Sutton gravitated to Kevin as unconsciously the man reminded him of his own father, only warmer and more assertive. Kevin was far less complex than Harry and far less troubled. Sutton began to favor him for this reason.

Kevin grew up on a farm in Iowa. He made it big in the film industry, spent a sizable chunk of his fortune on a ranch in Montana, and pined away his time in retirement waiting on grandchildren. As was fashionable for the last crop of movie stars that had been his contemporaries, he flew often to anti-aging clinics in Switzerland and Central America. He paid large sums to get the treatments and experimental medications that made his 70-year-old body appear 20 years younger. The agedness in his hands was the only tell.

The day came when Kevin was healed enough and riding with ease the horse Lucas had gifted him. He was training the horse to his preferences and learning the horse's personality in a five-acre fenced pasture as Sutton watched on, unable to decide whether the book in his hands or Kevin's horse training merited his attention more. Mary Lou rang the lunch bell in the distance. The men on the ranch all moved in unison to the picnic tables set under a beautiful timber-framed gazebo. Kevin was the last to join. Lucas led the group in prayer. Harry took only a few short bites and left to patrol the property as was his custom at every meal.

"I think I'll be leaving," said Kevin. "They haven't come back for me and I'm well enough to clear out in case they do. No harm will come to you if I'm gone."

"Fair enough," said Lucas, thinking of his family.

"I'm going with him," said Sutton. Only Greg was the least bit surprised. "I know you'll need my help in the fall—"

"It's fine," said Lucas. "Harry's a great help. We'll miss you, son."

"Don't be too long," said Mary Lou with a knowing look, referring to the birth of a child neither she nor her husband wanted Sutton to miss.

Sutton and Kevin rode out that same day. Lucas gifted Sutton an M24 rifle, so on either side of his saddle he bore rifles.

Kevin had with him the rifle he had ridden in with and a pair of pistols in a leather shoulder holster that glistened in the sun. They would ride to North Fork to stay with Milo and his wife. The cabin was nestled in the dry hills above the Salmon River just before the land turned green going into Montana. It served as the rendezvous for any disruption to the operation against the elite compound in Sun Valley. Kevin hoped to see Frank, Russell, and Horace, men he said he had seen escape alive.

They reached Kevin's property in four uneventful days, most of it on an overland route to avoid the highways and anyone who could potentially have the plague. Riding into the property they were horrified to see the cabin partly burned down. There were bodies strewn about in what had obviously been a one-sided firefight. Kevin leapt from his horse and Sutton followed suit. They barged into the home, Kevin shouting for Milo and Caroline, Milo's wife.

"Dad," came a beleaguered voice from a back bedroom.

They ran to the voice. Sutton tripped over a charred roof beam that had fallen onto the scored concrete floor. In the back bedroom they discovered Milo barely clinging to life. His face was badly bruised and swollen, his chest and legs bore bullet wounds, and all around him was a pool of blood. A large gash from a knife ran across his face as if the strike had been done in a rage. His left leg was mangled and cinched up tight with a belt.

"Dad," he repeated in a daze. His tremendous muscles looked withered from the blood loss. He wheezed as he spoke. "They took Caroline, Dad. The baby's due any time."

"How many were there, son?" Kevin asked as tears streaked down his face.

"Close to a dozen," he labored to say. "They came in the morning. Said they were on patrol. Said their leader was murdered. They spotted Frank and started shooting. Russell's over there. Frank and Horace were out when it started. I'm dying, dad," he said as his eyes welled up.

Kevin put his palm to his son's cheek.

"Which one did this to you?"

"The leader…"

Milo's breathing slowed down. The wheezing became more pronounced. "Held on as long as I could," he said with a pained smile. "They want the baby…" His face darkened. Death was near. "Save them, Dad." His eyelids slowly open and shut. With his remaining life he repeated, "Save them," and died.

Kevin sat next to the body of his only son for a time while Sutton walked around the property, taking stock of what had happened. Several hundred yards away down by the river he found the eviscerated bodies of two Satanists in their black uniforms, pinned under fallen horses covered in hundreds of flies. The body of a towering blonde man with a single bullet hole through his temple lay nearby, still clutching a rifle in his hands unlike any Sutton had seen before. The man's horse was shot to hell, still tethered to a tree. He pried the rifle from the man and shouldered it. He dragged into a ditch the bodies of who he presumed were neighbors that had come to help. They were all older folks, including two women. The air was silent save for the rush of the river some ways away. He set the rifle down against a wooden fence. He petted his horse to comfort himself, thinking of Milo's death and the death of the man he and Harry had put down on the road to Stanley.

Kevin emerged from the cabin when he was ready. His eyes were bloodshot and he carried the weight of death on his frame. He carried a bowie knife that measured the length of his forearm in a sheath across his chest. He bore a pair of grenades on his ammo belt around his waist. Sutton stepped toward him. He placed his hand on Sutton's shoulder and said, "You should go home."

"No, I'm riding with you," replied the young man.

A crackling of branches and the whinny of a third horse put them on alert and they trained their guns on the source of the sound. Frank thundered into view, his blue shirt soaked in blood and his horse complaining from a large wound in the bridge of its neck.

"They've got Caroline. Only one of them broke off to chase me. All I had was this," he showed them his spent pistol.

"Milo had me checking his traps down south when the shooting started. It must've been quick cause I engaged them out on the highway-" he stopped mid-sentence when he saw the cabin smoldering.

"How far out are they?" asked Kevin as he mounted his horse, motioning for Sutton to do the same.

"Maybe ten, twelve miles. One of their high priests is with them. That's got to be their last one. Brazen fucks."

"You still good to ride?"

"Oh yeah, this ain't my blood."

"They killed Russell and Milo," said Kevin.

Frank winced and put his hand to his chest. He thought of Russell's family back in Montana.

Kevin asked him, "We'll take them from either side of the highway, at a distance. You know where the vault is? Get what you need and let's get going. Sutton, toss down that rifle Lucas gave you and pick up the one setting against the fence. It's worth ten times as much."

"They're going slow but they know I'm around," said Frank as he emerged with a ballistic vest in place of his bloodied shirt. He placed a tremendous looking hunting rifle into a sleeve affixed to his horse's saddle. He tossed a second ballistic vest to

Kevin who refused it with a dead look in his eyes and gave it to Sutton.

They galloped out to the highway with Kevin in the lead. After a time, he motioned for them to slow down. Frank knew the highway and its features best as he had ridden down through Idaho on fishing trips every summer with his children. He told Sutton to ride hard along the eastern ridge overlooking the Salmon River until he met a craggy butte, called Tower Rock, overlooking an old state rest stop. He was to focus on the guards with the heaviest firepower and after two shots, Kevin and Frank would open up from a thicket of trees by the side of the highway.

Sutton rode his horse to its limit and made it to the butte far ahead of the enemy's procession. It was an hour before he could spot them through his scope. He marveled at the automatic adjustments his scope made, giving him a clue as to the special emphasis Kevin had placed on the weaponry. The procession kept up a steady trot. There were eight of them in addition to Caroline, who was seated atop an open cart with her legs bound to eye plates anchored to the floor of the cart. Her head hung heavy. He noticed people emerge from the only inhabited dwelling in sight. They were two men holding shotguns. They immediately set down their weapons when the procession trained its guns on them. Through his scope, Sutton could make out Kevin and Frank ride down from the western hills, crossing the river and tethering their horses behind a fence line before each took position at a different outhouse building situated at the dilapidated highway rest stop. The moment drew nearer as the enemy procession came onto the straight stretch that would lead them past the ambush point. Sutton calmed his breathing down and took a drink of water.

Sutton kept a bead on the uniformed guard that was still hold his light machine gun at attention from the earlier encounter with the two men and their shotguns. When the procession was nearly due east of him, he fired. The round detonated the man's chest instantly and tore into the blacktop of the highway. The guards yelled in surprise and took stock of their assailant's position. Sutton took bead and fired again, blowing the leg off of the guard seated in front Caroline. Automatic fire rained down on his position and the ominous hum of a drone came into his ears as he waited behind the rock to return fire. He drew out his sidearm just in time to gun down a drone that shot him once through the chest below the clavicle. The drone managed to disable his rifle in the exchange of fire. He heard further gunfire which pulled the enemy's attention away from his position. He pulled himself up to his feet to peak over the rock and reposition himself for another shot before he realized his rifle was out of commission.

Down below he saw Frank slump out from the side of outhouse on the south side of the rest stop as withering fire shredded his cover. Grenade explosions fell well short of Frank. Kevin put down the man that was laying heavy fire on Frank with a single shot through the head. The head exploded. Frank pushed himself back to cover, yelling something Sutton couldn't quite make out. The high priest, armed with only a sidearm, hopped down from his horse to run to Caroline and take her hostage but Kevin peaked out from cover and put a shot through the man's lower back. He dropped as if he were paralyzed. The remaining four guards split their fire between the two small buildings serving as cover. The element of surprise was lost and the firing was near continuous, the guards showing the merits of their training.

At this point, Sutton had shimmied his way down a steep gully and behind a broken tree. He managed to shoot one of the guards, wounding him grievously and pulling the pressure off of Kevin and Frank. Sutton was spotted and fired upon by the guards. A shot rang through his calf and he dropped to the ground, which saved his life as the tree was shredded to pieces. Kevin put down two of the guards with a grenade. The remaining guard growled as his rifle jammed. He went for his sidepiece but Kevin had already jumped the short fence and bridged the distance that remained between them. He grunted at the man, "Drop it," with his rifle fixed dead center on the man's chest. The man was a strange looking breed with hoop earrings through his ear lobes and facial surgeries that held none of their usual glamor as the long ride into the Idaho interior had precluded his customary use of makeup. In place of natural eyebrows, he bore pronounced ridges of skin pierced with a dozen rings. He took to his knees and crossed his hands behind his head.

The high priest was marked by wild hair colors and a slender feminine frame that contrasted with the hulking bodies

of the rest of the guards. He lay moaning on the asphalt. His face
was scorched red from the heat of the blacktop. Sutton limped
into view with his pistol.

"That one's still moving," Kevin said to Sutton,
indicating the guard he had shot from behind the tree earlier.
Sutton unceremoniously but a bullet through the man's skull,
wincing in disgust as the features of the face collapsed in on
themselves. He immediately turned his attention to Caroline,
who sobbed quietly with her face buried in her arms as she
crouched behind the sideboards of the wagon. She wouldn't let
him touch her, so he waited patiently to see what Kevin would
do. Frank ambled out from his cover, having seen Kevin and
Sutton up on the highway. Blood trickled from his ears and he
stumbled some as he came up to his friends and their two
surviving prisoners. He fixed his gun on the guard on his knees.

"You know how many of your kind are dying these
days?" Kevin asked as he kicked the paralyzed priest over onto
his back. "You made the world's fortune doing what you've
done." He said something to Frank but Frank replied that he
couldn't hear. He repeated what he said but to Sutton. Sutton
pulled the guard on his knees up to a standing position. He
patted down the guard, his face contorting in disgust as he felt no
genitalia on the guard's groan. He pulled a snub-nosed revolver
from the guard's ankle holster. Then he tied the guard to the
wagon, as far from Caroline as possible.

The ring of Kevin's bowie knife could be heard as he pulled it from its sheath and set his rifle on the ground in the same motion. He stood over the high priest of the child devouring cult and spoke, "You're the one who killed my son, back at the cabin."

The priest only smiled through bloody teeth.

"Your world order is dying. You plunged the earth into war and killed billions. Now you are hunted and your sins will be revisited upon you. I will have your heart. I send you back to Satan," he rumbled as he plunged his vast knife into the priest's chest and carved the heart out as the priest screamed, choked, and died. He wiped the knife clean on the priest's uniform, resheathed it, and place the dripping heart on the bench of the wagon while he tended to Caroline. He unlocked her chains with the key that was on the priest's belt and she collapsed into his arms. He held her and motioned to Frank to fetch their horses, including Sutton's up on the butte.

Caroline watched with glassy eyes as Kevin built a fire with the help of the two neighboring men who arrived with their shotguns in hand. Their women tended to Sutton, who was the most injured. They said could endure the ride back to North Fork but no further. The neighbors stayed behind to burn the dead guards, absent their uniforms which were piled into the back of the wagon. They took all but one of the surviving horses and all of the weaponry and provisions from the wagon as Kevin wanted nothing to do with anything of the sort.

Kevin, his people, and his prisoner went back to his cabin outside of North Fork to properly bury Milo, Russell, Horace, and the others who had died in the firefight. Kevin stood by as the surviving guard dug the graves. When the burials were finished, Sutton stayed behind with Caroline and a neighbor woman who had lost her husband on site while Kevin and Frank led the guard away to a barn at the edge of the property. There they tore the guard's shirt off, tied him down, and burned a Christian cross into his tattoo-covered back using heated steel irrigation pipes. Deep into the night they chopped the man's pointer and middle fingers off, cauterizing the stumps and taking their time so the man wouldn't die of shock. They tended to the mark on his back with a betadine solution. As morning broke, they knocked the man unconscious and put a bleach solution into his right eye. They treated the eye by washing it out and giving it antiseptic as the man came to. He screamed into his gag as he realized he had been blinded. They bound him to a wagon with the same chains that had been used on Caroline and hitched the horse that they'd kept for themselves from the neighbors. The uniforms of the satanic cult were affixed to the sides of the wagon.

Frank rode north to be with his family and to help Russell's family grieve. Sutton stayed with Caroline and the neighbor woman. Kevin slept for half of the day and then rode south alongside the wagon bearing his prisoner. He traveled to Salmon where he displayed his prisoner in the city park to the several hundred people who inhabited the town. The local sheriff, a man with a thick grey mustache and sunglasses that had gone out of style thirty years prior, approached Kevin.

"No need to take him that far south yourself, Mr. Tedrick," he said. "My deputies and I will take him to where he needs to go. The way is clear of plague."

"I want him to go back to his outfit *alive*," said Kevin. "He is an example for all to see."

The sheriff nodded, which was enough for Kevin – he was too troubled to entertain any of the obvious awe the townspeople held him in. He withdrew a tin containing the priest's heart from a saddlebag and set it on the wagon near the disfigured eunuch. "Make sure they get this, too. If there's enough of them left, tell them they can find me in Montana."

"One of your men is here. We know what you've been up to," said the sheriff. "We stand with you. Those people down in Sun Valley will get the message. There aren't too many of them left, I'd imagine."

The sheriff had one of his deputies lead Kevin to the small medical clinic where Erick from Alberton was lying in a hospital bed, recovering from the assault on the compound in Sun Valley. His left forearm had been shattered and as there was not the medical capabilities to save it, it had to be amputated. He and Kevin shared a warm conversation. Erick would visit him on his way north once he was well again.

Kevin returned to his cabin at North Fork. Sutton greeted him and brought him in to meet his grandson. Weeks passed. Sutton healed from his wounds. Kevin and Caroline mended their broken hearts at Milo's passing with the presence of a wonderful new life in their family. They rode north when the baby was ready.

On the highway leading steeply through Lolo Pass and toward Kevin's ranch, Kevin and Sutton were in conversation. There was a forest fire many miles away and thin smoke wafted through their surroundings.

"They'll need you in Stanley," said Kevin. "Plenty to harvest, plenty to do."

"I'll go back before too long."

"I could use you at my place," said Kevin, looking over to the man he'd become so fond of in such a short time.

"Would Milo accept it?" Sutton alluded to his budding interest in Caroline, which he did not hide from Kevin. In the weeks it had taken her to recover from childbirth, Sutton had spent more and more time by her side in conversation. He bore the burden of the death of her husband in helping her to grieve. He knew nearly the entirety of their years together and the many nuances of their marriage path. Caroline's intellect, virtue, and obvious beauty had fascinated him in a way that softened his heart toward the female species. Her goodness was inborn.

"Milo would. Caroline will, too, in time. You're hearty stock, Sutton. I'll raise the boy as my own. You understand, don't you?"

"I do."

He looked back into the wagon where Caroline was sleeping under cover with her boy held tight to her. Something in him relaxed in a way he had not felt since he was a boy.

Sutton married Caroline and she bore him six children. He spent his years traveling back and forth to Stanley, helping build up the people he knew. The lure of the library there had also proven too strong to keep him away for more than a winter. Kevin died twenty years later in his sleep with a smile on his face. Sutton lived to see civilization come back into the world.

He learned that his bloody excursion had been repeated all around the globe by thousands of brave-hearted people.

Made in the USA
Monee, IL
14 January 2021

57619593R00121